HERBERT'S WORMHOLE

THE RISE AND FALL OF EL SOLO LIBRE

HERB WORN

THE RISE AND FALL

Peter Nelson

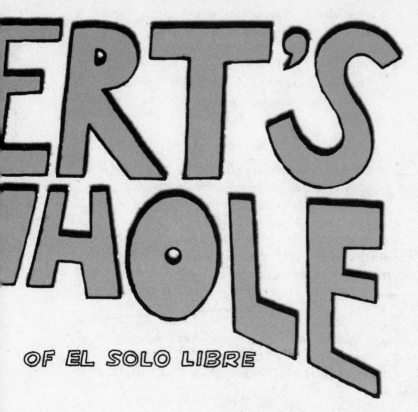

ERT'S WHOLE

OF EL SOLO LIBRE

Rohitash Rao

HARPER
An Imprint of HarperCollinsPublishers

To Christopher and your super-mega silly imagination
that goes to infinity, plus one.
—P. N.

To my favorite drawing partner (who also happens to be
my wonderful niece), Adriana Catalina Rao.
—R. R.

Herbert's Wormhole: The Rise and Fall of El Solo Libre
Copyright © 2012 by Peter Nelson and Rohitash Rao
All rights reserved. Printed in the United States of America.
No part of this book may be used or reproduced in any manner
whatsoever without written permission except in the case of brief
quotations embodied in critical articles and reviews. For information
address HarperCollins Children's Books, a division of HarperCollins
Publishers, 10 East 53rd Street, New York, NY 10022.
www.harpercollinschildrens.com

Library of Congress Cataloging-in-Publication Data
Nelson, Peter.
   The rise and fall of El Solo Libre / Peter Nelson & Rohitash Rao. —
1st ed.
       p.   cm. — (Herbert's wormhole)
   Summary: Pretending to be alien slayers when they travel via a
wormhole to their hometown 100 years in the future, ten-year-olds
Alex, Herbert, and Sammi must pull together when an actual alien
invasion occurs.
   ISBN 978-0-06-201218-0
   [1. Time travel—Fiction.   2. Extraterrestrial beings—Fiction.
3. Friendship—Fiction.]   I. Rao, Rohitash.   II. Title.
PZ7.N43583Ri 2012   2011022936
[Fic]—dc23

Typography by Alison Klapthor
12 13 14 15 16   CG/RRDH   10 9 8 7 6 5 4 3 2 1
❖

First Edition

FIRST, A WORD FROM OUR HEROES . . .

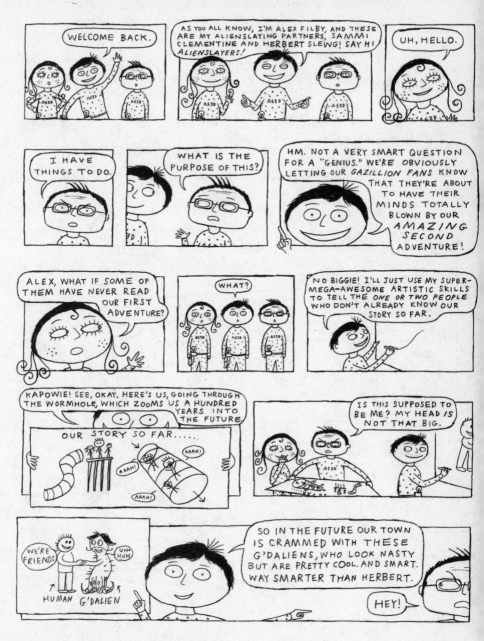

Alex Filby tapped his foot impatiently as he watched his dad aim a blaster at the very last Alien Invader.

"Watch this, son! I'M GONNA BLOW THIS SLIME-SUCKING FREAK INTO A GAZILLION SPACE-CHUNKS!"

Alex looked from his dad's grinning, unshaven face to the TV. *There's something weirdly familiar about this,* he thought.

FRZZZT!

His dad's grin sank. His blaster dropped to the

floor. The Alien Invader on the TV belched out an evil laugh. *"BWAH HAW HAW!! YOU HAVE BEEN DESTROYED, HUMAN! PLAY AGAIN?!?"*

"He got me," Mr. Filby whimpered, his lower lip trembling. "I was so close to beating the game, and then . . . *he fried me.*"

"Sorry 'bout that, Dad. Well, I gotta run."

"Wait!" Mr. Filby turned to him. "Where are you going? Help me fight the Leacacosian Lizard Emperor!"

Alex put a hand on his father's shoulder. "We've talked about this, Dad. Summer vacation's almost over, and I don't have many days left to play outside with my friends."

Mr. Filby nodded sadly.

"Besides," Alex continued, "I'm not into video games, remember?"

"Right," Alex's dad mumbled as his son rushed out of the room. "I guess I forgot."

Mr. Filby got hooked on AlienSlayer 2 soon after his wife had suggested he hook it up and try playing it with Alex. Although she once worried that her son spent too much time indoors playing the video game, she now worried her son was spending too much time *outdoors*, playing some silly spaceman fantasy game that seemed to involve dressing up in silver costumes and disappearing for hours with his neighbors, Herbert Slewg and Sammi Clementine.

Mrs. Filby worried a lot.

It *was* a little strange. All summer long, the three 10-year-olds would meet in the morning at Alex's backyard jungle gym, and Mrs. Filby wouldn't see her son again until it got dark. She much preferred being able to check in on her son every seven and a half minutes or so, even if it meant him sitting in front of the TV for hours, like he used to.

Unfortunately, the only thing her plan had accomplished was getting *Mr. Filby* hooked. As for her son, it was as if he had no memory of ever liking video games at all. (This may have been because earlier that summer Alex had accidentally erased the part of his brain that remembered ever liking video games at all.)

But even if that hadn't happened, Alex still would've chosen to go on his daily adventures with Herbert and Sammi rather than play AlienSlayer 2. Why would he want to *play* AlienSlayer when he actually *was* one?

Weeks earlier, Alex and his friends had discovered in his jungle gym a wormhole, or time-travel tunnel. It connected them to their same hometown, but a hundred years in the future. Once there, they foiled the evil plot of a very grumpy G'Dalien, convincing everyone in Future Merwinsville that they were AlienSlayers, with incredible alien-slaying powers.* Herbert and Sammi knew that they weren't *really* AlienSlayers, but the entire human and (mostly friendly) G'Dalien population of Future Merwinsville *believed* that they were.

And so did Alex.

---

*Which, technically, they weren't.

Alex locked his bedroom door behind him and pulled his Negative Energy Densifyer suit out of his bedroom closet. This computer-wired, all-silver bodysuit was Herbert's greatest invention (so far). The N.E.D. suit opened the wormhole, allowing its wearer to travel through time without being crushed, turned inside out, or instantly atomized into a billion teensy bits. It was also very shiny, and happened to look extremely awesome on Alex.

He zipped up his N.E.D. suit, puffed out his chest, and did his best superhero-actiony pose in the mirror. He flipped the tiny switch on the suit's belt buckle. All the little lights on his suit blinked to life and all the little wires connecting circuits and computer chips hummed and vibrated. He switched it back off, put his fists on his hips, and took one last look at himself. "Equipment, check.

Breakfast, check. Teeth brushed, check. Time to go to work, AlienSlayer. Your fans await."

He swung the door open, leaped out of his room in a single bound—and bumped into his mother. Mrs. Filby was holding a glossy, colorful brochure.

"There's my Snookybuns!" (Alex hated when she called him stuff like that, but at least this time there were no witnesses.) "Going outside to play your spaceman game with your little pals again?"

"Yeah, Mom," Alex said. "And I'm kinda late, so—"

"Sweetie, I know I'm the one who encouraged you to play outdoors more. And I realize I introduced you to your neighbor and new best friend, little *Herbie Slewg.*"

Alex wondered which would annoy Herbert more, being referred to as "little Herbie Slewg" or as Alex's best friend. Herbert considered himself a genius, and generally didn't consider many people worthy of his friendship. Which was fine with many people.

"But *Snugglekins,* you spend an awful lot of time playing this dress-up game," his mom continued. "I just wonder if it's, well, *normal behavior.*"

If you only knew, Alex thought. But that's not what he said.

"Well, we're imaginative kids, Mom," Alex heard himself say. "We're just developing early social skills by expressing our basic identities through dramatic role play."

Alex had no idea what he had just said, but apparently it worked. His mom grinned, then suddenly remembered the brochure she held in her hand. She thrust it in front of him. It had a bunch of pictures of smiling kids at summer camp, looking way too happy given what they were being forced to do—march single file through the woods, huddle together around smoky campfires, sleep on the ground. . . .

Ugh, Alex thought. It looked *awful*.

"It's a summer sleepover camp right down the street, at Merwinsville Public Park!" she said. "Doesn't it look fun?"

Alex studied his mother's face. She had that crazy gaze she had whenever she found something she thought would *enrich* him. He knew just how to handle this.

"Wow, Mom!" he blurted. "I'd love to take

7

personal responsibility and carefully consider this in a thoughtful and independent way! Can I, Mom? *Can I pleeeaaase?*"

"Of course you can, Bootlecakes!" Mrs. Filby smiled as she straightened a wrinkle on his N.E.D. suit. "Now you go 'blastoff' with your friends!"

Alex watched her bounce down the hallway. He crumpled up the brochure, chucked it into his very messy room, and headed for the backyard to meet his fellow AlienSlayers.

CHAPTER 2

Sammi Clementine hung upside down on the monkey bars of the jungle gym, her long pigtails nearly touching the ground. In her N.E.D. suit, she looked like a giant silver dangly earring.

"Seven forty-two," a voice spat. "He's precisely twelve minutes late. In three minutes I say we go through without him."

Sammi stared at Herbert Slewg. Even upside down, wearing an N.E.D. suit that resembled baggy, tinfoil pajamas, somehow he still didn't look silly. Herbert almost always looked serious.

"Relax. He'll be here." She began swinging back and forth. "Besides, it was your rule that we only go through the wormhole together, remember?"

Sammi launched herself from the monkey bars, did a double backflip, and landed on her feet. Herbert didn't notice. He just continued to stare at his watch.

"You sure that thing is even right?" she asked.

Herbert snorted loudly and held up his wristwatch. "This *thing* happens to be the standard issue atomic timepiece designed by the physicists at the European Organization for Nuclear Research in Geneva, Switzerland, home of the highest-energy synchrotronic particle accelerator in the world, capable of colliding opposing beams at one-point-one-two microjoules per particle. I think it can accurately tell the *time of day*."

"Wow, Switzerland." Sammi smiled. "That's where they make those pretty cuckoo clocks, isn't it?"

Herbert sneered at her and checked the time again.

"Seven forty-*three*."

"What's your hurry, anyway? Got a date with the future?"

"Yes, as a matter of fact. The future *me*."

Earlier that summer, when they first traveled to the future, Herbert had the odd pleasure of meeting his older self—a 110-year-old Herbert Slewg.

"That's gotta be kinda weird," Sammi said. "Hanging out with the future old man version of yourself, I mean."

"Of course it's not *weird*. I grew up to become an exceptional scientist and inventor, just as I expected."

"I have no interest in meeting my future self. However I turn out, I want it to be a surprise. Plus, it seems kinda dishonest. Like getting the answers ahead of the test."

"I've *never* needed the answers to *any* test ahead of time." Herbert glared at her for a second. "Anyway, I'm glad you feel that way, because it's better if you don't. Any contact you or Alex have with your future selves could negatively affect everyone you've ever met—or have yet to meet."

"So why is it safe for you?"

"I don't know if you've noticed, but I'm not much of a people person. Unlike *you two*, I don't run around *befriending* every single resident of

Merwinsville I pass in the street."

Sammi thought for a moment. "Have you ever thought maybe we should tell everyone the truth? Y'know—*that we're not really AlienSlayers?*"

Herbert squinted at her. "Publicly announcing the truth would have an even *more* immediate negative effect on the people and G'Daliens of Merwinsville—shock, fear, chaos, not to mention intense hatred toward us. Please think before you speak."

"It's just that when we first tricked everyone, it was to save the world and get the people and G'Daliens to live together in peace. That was a good thing. But now they treat us like superheroes, which we're not. It's like we're *lying to everybody.* Don't you feel guilty knowing we don't deserve all that fame and glory? That we're just normal, boring kids?"

Herbert put a hand on his chin and thought for a moment.

"No."

"Why am I not surprised."

"Because as usual, I'm thinking rationally. I don't care about being a celebrity, so therefore I feel no guilt. I care about science, about technology, about inventing. And I know if everyone in the future were to suddenly find out we were just 'normal, boring kids,' all the amazing stuff the G'Daliens have given us to watch for an alien invasion— our lab, our equipment, our incredibly advanced supercomputer—it would all go away."

"And that makes it worth living a lie?"

"Please. For science? I'd do cartwheels down Main Street of Future Merwinsville wearing a wig, lipstick, and a flowery dress."

Sammi tried to scrub that image from her brain. Herbert continued. "And let's not pretend you don't enjoy the perks of the job yourself."

"What do you mean?"

"Chicago, that dimwitted future boy who likes you so much."

"*Hey!* Don't call Chicago dim— *Wait.* You think he likes me?" Sammi's face began to turn a pinkish-red. Chicago Illinois was a kid in the future who knew the truth about them and helped them sneak in and out of the wormhole. Sammi thought he was kind of *okay*, but tried not to let it show. Especially to him.

"This is not my field of expertise, but I'd postulate that he likes the fame, the cheering crowds, the mayor's car, the free smoothies, and you—in that order."

"All right, all right." Sammi cut him off sharply. She really didn't want to think about how far down she was on the list of things Chicago liked, especially today, the day he was taking her out for pizza and ice cream. "I guess there's no harm in letting Merwinsvillians believe they have their very own AlienSlayers for a *little* while longer. But I do feel we should at least tell Alex."

"Ill-advised and potentially dangerous," Herbert deduced. "He'd never be able to keep it a secret from the Merwinsvillians. Besides, it was you who said we should let him 'live the dream.'"

"I know, but he's *actually* living the dream. He's gotta hear the truth sooner or later, and he's so into it I'm worried it'll crush him. I think it's our responsibility to tell Alex."

"Tell me what?"

Sammi and Herbert spun around. Alex was standing beside the jungle gym ladder.

Herbert shot Sammi a look. She thought quickly.

"Uh, that you're late," she said. "And Herbert was considering going through the wormhole without you."

"*What?*" Alex stepped up to Herbert and got in his face. "You can't do that! Everyone goes through together, or no one does! Sound familiar? It's *your* rule, Ruley McRulemaker!"

Sammi climbed the ladder and stood on the tube slide platform. She watched Alex and Herbert argue, and wondered why she had just lied to her friend.

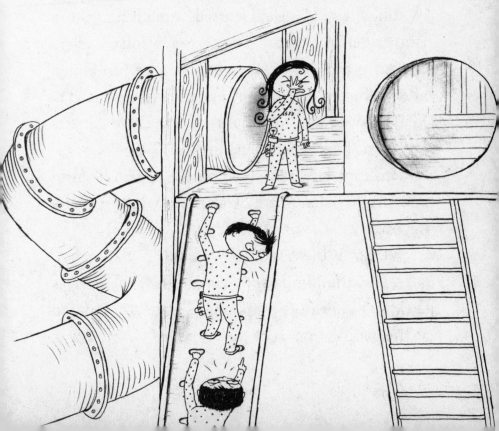

"I don't remember electing you the boss!" Alex said.

"Well, maybe you'll remember that you're in my N.E.D. suit!"

"Well, maybe *you'll* remember you're on *my* jungle gym!"

They fought their way to the top and joined Sammi in front of the gaping mouth of the blue tube slide.

"C'mon, you guys," she said. "Let's just get to work."

"She's right." Alex started stretching like a runner before a race. "Time to get serious. Today's the day. I can feel it. We're gonna get a full-blown alien invasion today! The entire town's gonna look to us to save them, and that's when the AlienSlayers are gonna kick some alien butt! *Let's hit it!*"

He flipped the switch on his N.E.D. suit. Sammi and Herbert shared a look as they switched theirs on, too.

WUBBA-WUBBA-WUBBA-WUBBA!

A low, thudding sound rattled the tube slide as their suits began to blink and vibrate. They stared at the gaping mouth of the slide and watched as a strange, shimmery blue light grew brighter and began to bend inward. They felt themselves being pulled toward it.

WUBBA-WUBBA-WUBBA-WUBBA-WUBBA-WUBBA!!!

As the sound grew louder, the tugging got stronger and stronger. The silver-suited trio lined up like skydivers about to leap out of a plane. They took a deep breath and jumped.

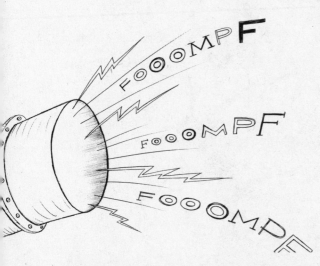

The noise stopped and the jungle gym went still. The shimmery blue wormhole vanished immediately after swallowing the three AlienSlayers.

$\mathbb{A}$ chubby, eight-tentacled, squidlike G'Dalien loomed over a group of young children. As she smiled, her bloodred lipstick parted to reveal a mouth full of razor-sharp teeth. The children let out loud screams—of delight.

"Right this way, my adorable little roos!" she said in a thick Australian accent, leading them through the Merwinsville Museum of Human History. "Come get a gander at the very first G'Dalien-human contact ever made, thousands and thousands of years ago!"

As they entered a long hallway, her giant beehive-hairdo wig seemed to float atop her blobby, greenish-gray head. She wore a tour guide vest with a large name tag that read, *"G'Day! My Name is: CA-ROL. Ask Me Anything!"* CA-ROL led the class of human and G'Dalien youngsters past the historical dioramas that made up the Hallway of Human History.

"OUTTA THE WAY!"

A panicked voice suddenly echoed through the long hall. A good-looking boy wearing a baseball cap and orange jumpsuit was recklessly steering what looked like a floating golf cart down the hall. Sitting in the back were Dallas, a big, beefy human, and Sausalito, a skinny, buglike kid. A bunch of signs and rods and cloth were jammed in the back of the AirCart.

SLAPSLAPSLAPSLAPSLAPSLAPSLAP

Running behind the cart was a short little G'Dalien named EL-ROY, who'd clearly missed his ride. His tentacles flapped against the shiny white floor as he scurried to catch up with his friends.

"*RUNNIN' LATE AND COMIN' THROUGH!*"

CA-ROL quickly herded the little ones to the side as Chicago and his orange-jumpsuited buddies zoomed past. They glided to a halt in front of a diorama. A group of fake cavemen sat beside a fake fire alongside a stuffed woolly mammoth, and a G'Dalien spaceship hung overhead. The driver of the cart leaped out, jumped the railing, and turned back to smile at the confused tour group.

"Sorry, kids! This part of the exhibit is temporarily closed!" He pointed to the name tag on his orange jumpsuit. It read, "Hello! My name is: CHICAGO ILLINOIS: EXHIBIT TECHNICIAN, MERWINSVILLE MUSEUM OF HUMAN HISTORY."

Sausalito jumped out and put up a large curtain, pulling it across the diorama. Printed on the curtain in huge block letters were the words: "*PLEASE PARDON OUR MESS!* EXHIBIT UNDER CONSTRUCTION." In front of that, Dallas quickly erected a large fencelike blockade with even huger block letters printed on it: "CAUTION! STAY BACK 300 FEET AT ALL TIMES." Finally, EL-ROY came flip-flopping up, squeaking to a stop. He crossed his arms and scowled at the confused children.

The youngsters looked up at CA-ROL, who looked just as befuddled as they were.

"*Right!*" she blurted out cheerfully. "Who's ready for a snickety-snack at the cafeteria, then? Let's move along now!" She shot back a look as she shuffled the kids down the hall.

Inside the caveman diorama, Chicago glanced at his watch, which looked remarkably similar to the one Herbert was bragging about. His eyes widened as a sparkling blue ripple began to appear in the center of a black-painted fake cave entrance.

POP! POP! POP! Herbert, Alex, and Sammi came flying out of the wormhole. Herbert flew past Chicago and stumbled a bit, barely keeping his balance as he slid to a stop—only to be knocked down by Alex, who popped out fanny-first and slammed into him. Sammi popped out last, somersaulting like a ninja and sliding into Chicago's arms. Chicago smiled at her.

Chicago left Dallas, Sausalito, and EL-ROY to reopen the caveman diorama as he taxied the AlienSlayers in the AirCart through the Merwinsville Museum of Human History. They passed exhibits and artifacts showing how the wise and friendly G'Daliens had come to Earth decades ago and saved the human race from near-extinction. In return for cleaning up a very messy planet and sharing their advanced alien technology, the G'Daliens were allowed to take over and run everything. Proof of a happy partnership wasn't just in the glass cases, behind the railings, and on the walls of the museum. It was also evident in the hallways, snack bars, and gift shops, where Humans and G'Daliens co-mingled like one big, happy, slightly weird-looking family.

As the AlienSlayers made their way toward the lobby, many members of this weird-looking family recognized them. Some smiled and pointed, others took pictures. Some followed at a respectful distance, and still more ran ahead of them excitedly.

"Okay, Chi-Town," Alex asked his driver. "Whaddya got lined up for us today?"

Chicago pressed a button on his wristwatch. A holographic checklist beamed out of it and hovered above his arm.

"You guys are gonna love this!" Chicago said, swerving to miss a G'Dalien woman trying to take their picture. "I've got a call in for you to do interviews with *Total Universal Inside Access: Merwinsville!* Cool, right?"

"No alien threats?" Alex asked.

"Nope."

"Any cosmic disturbances?"

"Uh-uh."

"Did a suspicious meteorite crash-land in the city and maybe sprout slimy vine-pods that drool acid when they come in contact with human flesh?"

"Sorry, Alex," Chicago said. "It's been pretty quiet since yesterday."

Alex slumped back in his seat. Sammi glanced at Herbert. Then she threw her arms around the two of them.

Chicago pulled up to the towering museum entrance doors. "We sure are! Along with a few friends!"

As the great museum doors began to open, a deafening *ROAR* broke out on the other side. Alex, Herbert, and Sammi stepped out to greet their fans. Gathered all the way down the long stone steps of the museum were thousands of Merwinsvillians—humans and G'Daliens alike—jumping, screaming, and holding giant banners for their hometown AlienSlayers.

Alex, Herbert, and Sammi waved to their fans as their AirCart glided slowly through the cheering crowd along the perfectly clean, shiny, plastic walk streets of downtown Future Merwinsville. They inched past the TransPort Station, a massive clump of clear sucker-tubes, which served as the quickest, easiest, hair-messingest mode of transportation around the city. They saw the gleaming G'Dalien buildings towering over their heads and countless G'Dalien technological wonders floating, flying, and skittering all around them as they approached the tallest building in all of Future Merwinsville—City Hall, home of the SlayerLair.

The AlienSlayers' homebase was located at the very tippity-top of City Hall—a lookout perched at the highest point in Merwinsville. The entrance was on the ground level and guarded by LO-PEZ, a heavyset G'Dalien who loved his job almost as much as he loved pizza, cupcakes, hot dogs, chips, and doughnuts. Which is what he had for a snack between most meals.

"All right, everybody," LO-PEZ belched through a mouthful of biscuits to the mob of people crowding the entrance. "Let 'em through. Let 'em through!"

Chicago helped LO-PEZ clear a path through the excited crowd of onlookers as Herbert, Alex, and Sammi pushed their way to the door. They boarded the all-glass, see-through SlayerVator that would shoot them up to their headquarters, hundreds of stories above the streets of Future Merwinsville.

Alex stepped back out for one last wave to the crowd.

"Thank you! We love you! See you soon!"

Herbert grabbed Alex by his collar and yanked him back inside the SlayerVator.

The doors *whooshed* shut and the SlayerVator shot upward, allowing two full seconds of quiet before reaching the 3,000th floor, high above the city.

Inside, the room was the perfect lookout spot for protecting an entire city from alien attack: floor-to-ceiling windows, plenty of comfortable seating, and a supercomputer who could tell them anything they needed to know, while making any kind of smoothie they could think of.

Alex burst into the room, rushed to the wall-sized supercomputer, and called out to it by name.

"SarcasmaTron, report! Any impending alien attacks?"

The highly advanced technological brain whirred and clicked. Its lights blinked and flashed as it computed its final answer.

"Oh, yeah . . . *tons of 'em,*" it said in a very smart-alecky voice. "The odds are a *tetraquadzillion-*to-one, so do the math."

"You're being sarcastic again, aren't you."

"SarcasmaTron computing answer . . . computing . . . computing . . . uh, yeah, *kinda.*"

Alex flopped himself down in a jelly-filled squishy chair. He really didn't like SarcasmaTron very much.

Sammi pulled up a barstool at SarcasmaTron's built-in smoothie bar. "Black raspberry, orange sherbet, bananas, and kiwi, please." A whirring was heard somewhere below the bar, followed by a soft *ding!* A panel slid open and a purplish-orange-yellowy-green frosty drink popped out.

"Oops. Whipped cream, please."

The drink dropped into the bar again and popped

back out half a second later. *Ding!* It was topped with a poofy head of whipped cream. Sammi smiled and took a big slurp of her smoothie.

Herbert crossed to an old man in an antigravity floating wheelchair, working on a complicated invention laid out on a table.

"Hey, good to see me!"

The AirChair spun around. Sitting in it was Herbert. Or, to be more exact, 110-year-old Herbert. His future self. Future Herbert wore glasses and had a similar expression to his younger self, just with a lot more wrinkles and a lot less hair.

"Greetings, boy genius!" the old man said. "How's the smartest person in Merwinsville today?"

"I was about to ask you the same question!"

As they both laughed together, Alex looked on. "I liked you two better when you hated each other."

"The odds of that dynamic remaining unchanged were highly unlikely," Old Man Herbert said.

"Predictably," Herbert added. "We have so much in common!"

"Precisely!"

The two Herberts high-fived. Alex turned his attention over to the smoothie bar. Chicago had arrived, and he had a straw in Sammi's smoothie. The two were slurping happily.

"Delicious!" He grinned.

As Sammi smiled back at Chicago, Alex stood up. "It's getting a bit too buddy-buddy in here. I'm gonna go downstairs and sign a few hundred autographs. Let me know if anything exciting happens—"

SLAM! SLAM! SLAM! SLAM!

Heavy titanium sheets suddenly dropped down over the windows of the SlayerLair, plunging the room into complete darkness.

"EVERYONE STAY EXACTLY WHERE THEY ARE. NOBODY MOVE!"

The voice boomed from over by the SlayerVator door. A bright green laser scanner cut through the darkness, sweeping the SlayerLair with its precise light, covering every nook and cranny of the room before retracting back to its source near the SlayerVator.

The lights came up and the window plates retracted. Standing there in a trench coat and old-timey hat was Chicago's dad, Mr. Illinois. He slipped his laser-pen into his coat pocket, lifted his wrist to his bushy mustache, and spoke into his sleeve.

"Room secure," he barked. "All clear. Send in M.O.M."

Sammi looked at Chicago. "*Mom?*"

"M.O.M.—Mayor of Merwinsville. It's a code-name Dad came up with," Chicago whispered. "He's been working on it ever since he was made Special Agent Head of Mayoral Security last month."

Special Agent Illinois stepped away from the door while keeping a suspicious eye on everyone in the room. A short, chubby, smiling G'Dalien burst in. "Greetings, AlienSlayers!"

Mayor CROM-WELL wasn't very big for a full-grown G'Dalien and might have been mistaken for a plump, overgrown G'Dalien baby if not for his sharp suit with vest, big bow tie, and shiny sash.

"How *fabulous* to find you hard at work, vigilantly watching over the good citizens of our fine city and protecting us from any and all uninvited intruders!"

The mayor smiled at everyone in the SlayerLair. His grin revealed a wall of perfectly straight, perfectly white, squared-off teeth. They were not at all like the rows of tiny pointed daggers common to his species, but rather like two rows of dice, without the dots.

"Actually, sir, there are no signs of alien invasion," Chicago said. "So I was going to line up an interview on *Total Universal Inside Access: Merwinsville!*"

"*Fantastic!* But first you must join me for our groundbreaking ceremony! We're building a state-of-the-art coliseum for the Great G'Dalien Flee-Festival this weekend, and I need my AlienSlayers to help me kick it off and fire up the crowd!"

Sammi, Alex, and Herbert looked at one another. Besides Mayor CROM-WELL, only one other person in the room seemed excited about the day's schedule.

Chicago fist-pumped the air. "*Awesome!*"

Sammi set down her smoothie and approached Mayor CROM-WELL. "Sorry, sir, but what exactly is a Great G'Dalien Fly Festival?"

Mayor CROM-WELL's jaw dropped open. For the first time ever, he was speechless. But he quickly recovered.

"*Flee*-Festival! It's only the most important historical event in G'Dalien history!"

Old Man Herbert knew what was coming. He turned and addressed the wall-sized computer. "SarcasmaTron, commence flashback simulation."

"Of course," the sassy-voiced supercomputer spat back. "Because he couldn't just *tell* them the story."

The lights inside the SlayerLair dimmed. SarcasmaTron's HoloScreen beamed a 3-D image into the center of the room. Herbert, Alex, and Sammi looked up at a peaceful-looking planet they didn't recognize. The G'Dalien mayor began narrating in his most dramatic voice.

"This was once our planet. Like your Earth, it was not without its problems. But it was home."

WHOOSH! In an instant, the holographic planet was suddenly surrounded by holographic spaceships. Not doughnut-shaped, friendly looking, little UFO-type spaceships, but pointy, menacing-looking battle cruiser–type spaceships.

"Then came . . . *the Klapthorians.* The bullies of our galaxy."

"Oh, no!" Sammi gasped. "What did they want?"

"They wanted . . . *our LUNN-CHMUNNY.*"

"Your *lunch money?*" Herbert blurted.

"You're kidding us, right?" Alex asked.

40

"I know, I know, it sounds similar." The mayor rolled his eyes as if he'd explained this thousands of times before. "But it's pronounced *LUNN-CHMUNNY*, not 'lunch money.' Totally different. It's one of the most rare and valuable substances in the known universe. Now, may I finish?"

"Please," SarcasmaTron spat. "The suspense is *killing* us."

"Thank you. So the Klapthorians attacked our defenseless planet with their massive Death Cruisers, stealing each and every G'Dalien's LUNN-CHMUNNY."

Sammi giggled into her smoothie.

Alex sat up and threw a few air punches. "Cool! And that's when you fought back, right?!"

Mayor CROM-WELL smiled at him. "Of course not! We did what G'Daliens do best. We fled! We fled proudly and with great speed, racing away nobly across the galaxy!"

The HoloScreen showed tiny little spaceships pathetically popping off the overrun G'Dalien planet.

Then the lights came up.

"That's it?!" Sammi blurted.

"*That's* what you celebrate?" Herbert asked in disbelief.

"That is so lame," Alex said.

The mayor smiled at them. "We had to protect our youngsters, as well as our peaceful heritage. Fighting would have risked both, so we chose to flee. I suppose to three mighty warriors such as yourselves, that would seem . . . '*lame.*'"

"Yep, too bad you didn't have us around back then," Alex said, karate-kicking his defenseless jelly-filled squishy chair.

"Precisely my point!" The mayor continued, "Had we not fled those fifty years ago, we would not have discovered such great friendships here on Earth. And to G'Daliens, that is what is most important. True friendship is worth more than all the LUNN-CHMUNNY in the universe."

The others looked at one another, and tried not to laugh.

The large circular clearing at the far end of Main Street had been slowly filling up with Merwinsvillians for most of the morning. By the time Mayor CROM-WELL's personal TransPodium appeared in the sky with Herbert, Alex, and Sammi aboard, the scene below had grown into an enormous pep rally.

The mayor's TransPodium was a small, anti-gravity stage that flew him from event to event. It was conveniently equipped with a voice-amplification unit so that thousands of citizens could hear his speeches, large MonitOrb screens so they could see him up close, and multiple firework cannons so they knew when to clap.

The mayor pointed down at the vast site. "This is where we are building the *Flee-a-seum*, an enormous arena with stadium seating, overlooking a beautifully landscaped open field."

"What happens on the field?" Herbert asked.

"The Great G'Dalien Flee-Festival!" The mayor gestured grandly. "On the fiftieth anniversary of the Great G'Dalien Fleeing, every citizen in Merwinsville will take part in a symbolic re-enactment!"

"You mean, they'll *flee*?" Sammi asked.

"Precisely! G'Daliens will run in mock-terror down Main Street, mock-fleeing from a mock-Klapthorian Winged Death Slug. When the terrified G'Daliens enter the Flee-a-seum, all of Merwinsville's human population will rise from their seats and chant, 'Welcome, G'Dalien Friends! Please take control of our planet in exchange for all your marvelously advanced gifts!'"

They all stared at the grinning mayor, unimpressed.

The TransPodium descended, hovering just above the crowded center of the circle. Merwinsvillians cheered so loudly Sammi had to cover her ears. Special Agent Illinois suspiciously scanned the audience for any sign of troublemakers. He gave the all-clear sign. The mayor stepped up and addressed his people.

"Greetings G'Daliens, Humans, Merwinsvillians all!"

The crowd roared back. Mayor CROM-WELL held up a tentacle.

"Today we break ground on what will be the site of much jubilation—the first ever *Great G'Dalien Flee-Festival!* This weekend we invite all of you to take part in reenacting the hastily heroic retreat we G'Daliens made fifty years ago and the warmly tentative welcome we found once we arrived here on Earth!"

Herbert and Sammi glanced at each other. *This weekend?* The stadium hadn't even been built yet. It was just a big empty space.

Alex was in awe of the audience. It was the biggest crowd of Merwinsvillians he'd ever seen gathered together for something that wasn't about him.

Mayor CROM-WELL gestured to the three of them to step forward. "Here to help kick off the commencement of our shrine to this great event are Merwinsville's very own *ALIENSLAYERS!*"

Chicago ushered them toward the front of the TransPodium, clearing the way. Herbert and Sammi were nearly trampled by Alex, who leaped in front of them. He threw his arms open as if trying to give the entire crowd a giant bear hug.

"Thank you!" Alex bellowed so loudly his voice was cracking. *"We love you, Merwinsville!"* He blew kisses to the crowd.

Herbert was seriously considering pushing him off the TransPodium into his beloved admirers, until a strange noise distracted him.

"BOO! BOOO!"

Herbert looked around. Alex and Sammi heard it, too. They glanced down into the front row, directly beneath the TransPodium. Standing there giving them a nasty look was a shabby, mean-looking G'Dalien with a terrible attitude. It was GOR-DON, the bitter blob whose evil plot they'd foiled earlier that summer. He was pulling flyers out of a soiled bag draped over his shoulder and handing them to people who clearly didn't want them. He wore a stained T-shirt.

"*That's right! BOO! SERIOUSLY, BOO!!!* Listen to me! The AlienSlayers are phonies! They're fakes! I have proof—*BEHOLD!*"

He pulled out of his bag a beat-up old cardboard box. Herbert recognized it immediately. Sammi gasped. Special Agent Illinois dove into action.

"HE'S GOING FOR A WEAPON! *M.O.M. IN DANGER! SWARM! SWARM!*" He tackled Mayor CROM-WELL to the floor of the TransPodium and bounced onto the stumpy G'Dalien's belly, keeping his balance on top of him as he looked around frantically. Just offstage, GOR-DON was being lifted up by the crowd.

"AAAUUUGGGHHH!!" the bald G'Dalien yowled. "LET GO OF ME!"

Herbert and Sammi knew GOR-DON hadn't pulled out a weapon. He'd pulled out something far more alarming—the box from a 100-year-old AS:3D! video game they'd used to defeat him and trick the entire town of Merwinsville into thinking they were real AlienSlayers.

Alex spotted it, too, but couldn't put his finger on what that box reminded him of. *There's something weirdly familiar about this*, he thought to himself as he watched the crowd pass GOR-DON back.

"WHAT ARE YOU DOING?! PUT ME DOWN! STOP THIS!" The enraged G'Dalien growled and squirmed, his protests growing fainter and fainter as he bounced over everyone's head and was finally

tossed out onto his blobby butt.

Mr. Illinois shouted into his sleeve as he rolled off his boss. *"ALL CLEAR! M.O.M. IS OUT OF DANGER!"*

Mayor CROM-WELL stumbled to his feet and gathered himself. "That wasn't on today's program," he muttered. He cleared his throat and addressed the crowd again. *"Now then!* Let the great Flee-a-seum groundbreaking begin!"

The crowd went wild as the TransPodium floated over to a giant golden shovel, its handle as thick as a telephone pole, suspended above the ground. The mayor nodded to Alex, Herbert, and Sammi. The three of them approached the enormous, shiny spade. The mayor led the crowd in a countdown.

"FIVE! FOUR! THREE! TWO! ONE!"

The AlienSlayers reached out and touched the golden shovel. It began to hum as it automatically sunk into the ground below. The handle opened with a *whirr.* Metal scaffolding folded out like mechanical arms and began snapping into place. The crowd watched as ramps, stairs, bleachers, and seats self-constructed all around them. Within seconds an entire Flee-a-seum, with seating for tens of thousands, was completed.

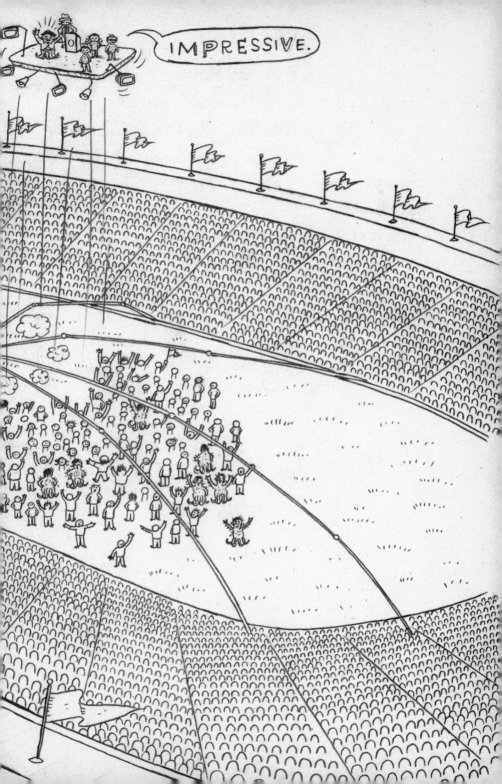

"Okay, I guess that's it," the mayor announced. "See you all on Saturday, and remember—gates open at noon, rain or shine. No cans, glass bottles, or coolers of any kind. And don't forget the sunscreen for your specific flesh type. *Thank you, Merwinsville!*"

Mayor CROM-WELL flashed his big wall of teeth. He wrapped his tentacles around the AlienSlayers, waving to the crowd as the TransPodium lifted them up, up, and away, into the blue sky.

CHAPTER 8

GOR-DON was still fuming angrily to himself as he rode down an empty Main Street in his broken-down floating jalopy.

His junky scrap-car endlessly announced to no one: "*ALIENSLAYERS ARE FAKES! ASK ME HOW I KNOW!*" It blared all the way across town, "*DON'T BE FOOLED! THE ALIENSLAYERS ARE PHONIES! READ MY PAMPHLET & LEARN THE TRUTH!*" The rickety vehicle spewed out flyers, littering the otherwise perfectly spotless street. Small ClutterBots whirred behind him, scooping up the flyers, disintegrating them as soon as they hit the ground, while he continued to the edge of town, toward the Merwinsville Museum of Human History.

GOR-DON was once head janitor of the museum, but that was before Sammi, Alex, and Herbert ruined his life. He now lived in a small closet in the museum basement. It was from this damp, smelly room that he'd been planning revenge on his archenemies ever since. At least when he wasn't napping.

GOR-DON parked his vehicle, entered the basement, and slinked around the huge Trash Disintegration Unit in the center of the floor.

He came to a door marked *KEEP OUT! TOXIC CONTAMINANT CLOSET!*

"Home sweet home," he mumbled as he opened the door.

Inside, the walls were stained, dirty, and bare. The dark, dank room was mostly empty except for a mangy cot, a desk along the wall, and a pile of Andretti's Pizzeria boxes stacked by the door. GOR-DON shuffled over to the beat-up computer on the desk. He went to switch it on, but stopped to pick up a framed picture.

It was a photograph of a chubby lady wearing a hairnet, holding up a spatula. GOR-DON sighed before snapping out of his trance. He put the picture down and switched on the computer.

The screen gave the room an even spookier green glow, and a built-in projection unit atop the monitor blinked to life. GOR-DON stood back to look at the projected display now on the blank wall. A gallery of pictures, articles, and video clips floated before him like a big collage. Each one was a story about the same subject.

He seethed at all the happy stories about his enemies.

"All of these do-goody events just make everyone love them more. . . . I must find a way to *expose them for what they are . . .*"

Beep! The computer's soothing voice interrupted his scheming with an announcement. *"You've got issues! New item on topic of your unhealthy obsession. Accept or decline?"*

"Accept," GOR-DON spat.

An image of Herbert, Alex, and Sammi standing on the TransPodium with Mayor CROM-WELL popped up. The headline read: *"ALIENSLAYERS HELP*

MAYOR KICK OFF GREAT G'DALIEN FLEE-FESTIVAL!"
Beneath it, in smaller type, it said: *"Local Crackpot
Makes Fool of Himself Again, Gets Tossed Out on Blobby
Butt ..."*

"AARRGGH!!"

The angry G'Dalien ex-janitor flew into a rage.

He rushed the wall and punched the projected
picture. His balled-up tentacle slammed into solid

metal with a *CRUNCH!*

"*Owweeeee!*"

GOR-DON flopped onto the desk and blew on his throbbing fist. He opened his eyes and glanced at the wall of holo-clippings. Noticing something, he sat up. He reached out to the new article and enlarged the AlienSlayer picture. There was a good-looking boy in a baseball cap happily working behind the AlienSlayers.

GOR-DON moved the new picture aside and zoomed in on another. There was Chicago again, this time crouching behind them so that photographers could get a shot of the AlienSlayers. In still another, he spotted Chicago in the background, looking at a schedule on his holographic wristwatch.

GOR-DON excitedly flipped through the pictures faster and faster, sliding them around and zooming in on them. In almost every one, he found Chicago.

As he smiled, his craggy, yellow teeth glowed in the light of the projections.

"I think perhaps it's time the little man behind

the superstars got some 'special' attention," he sneered.

GOR-DON began to laugh louder and louder, until his desk shook and finally gave way beneath his hefty, jiggling belly.

Chicago held the door open to the SlayerLair for Alex, Herbert, and Sammi and congratulated them as they entered.

"Had to be your biggest crowd *ever*. I'll get the numbers and let you guys know."

Sammi watched Chicago punch away at his wristwatch.

"It's nice that the G'Daliens are celebrating their friendship with humans," she said. "But I don't get why they're proud of how they gave up their home planet and ran from a bunch of space bullies."

"Yeah," said Alex. "I wish that rather than reenact how they wussed out, they'd invite those Cashmerians to that coliseum *for real*, so we could kick their butts, AlienSlayer-style!"

"It's *Klapthorians*," Old Man Herbert said. He was floating in his AirChair, making some much-needed attitude adjustments to SarcasmaTron. "It's an important part of their history."

Alex turned his attention to Old Man Herbert. "Speaking of history, since you're Herbert, you've already gone through this. You must know what happens to us. What's the deal? Do we *ever* get to fight aliens again?"

The 110-year-old inventor turned his AirChair around to face Alex. "It doesn't work that way. Unlike you three, I reached this exact moment one day at a time, one month at a time, one year at a time. In short, I did it 'old school,' as the kids used to say. *I aged*."

"Okay," Alex said. "So you didn't go through a wormhole like we did. But you still came from the same place, *before* the wormhole." His face lit up suddenly. "Which means you had to have known me! So what happened to me? Where'd my old-guy version end up?"

There was a long pause. "This is not a wise conversation to have," Young Herbert suddenly said. "We should stop."

"*What?!*"

Alex jumped to his feet and marched straight at Herbert. "So *you* get a cool old dude version of yourself but I *don't*? What's that, another one of your 'pre-agreed terms'?!"

Before Herbert could answer, Chicago broke in excitedly.

"Hey, great news, you guys! I just spoke with a reporter from the *Total Universal Inside Access: Merwinsville!* show, and they want to talk to me about an exclusive AlienSlayer interview! Isn't that great?"

"Uh, no offense," Sammi said. "But why do they want to meet with *you*?"

"She said she wanted to get some background info before the interview, from the 'hero behind the heroes.' That's me! Awesome, right?!"

"Yeah. Awesome," Sammi said, trying not to sound disappointed. "I guess we can grab pizza and ice cream some other time."

"Oh! I totally forgot. But let's face it—this is a little more important than pizza and ice cream, am I right? See you guys! I've gotta go change my shirt—maybe I'll be on TV!"

Chicago ran out of the room, leaving an awkward silence, until Alex cleared his throat. "Hey, I'll go grab some pizza with you if—"

"Forget it," Sammi said, storming over to the smoothie bar. "I'm not hungry anyway." She ordered a smoothie—for one—and slumped into a seat. Alex watched her. He seemed annoyed, and looked like he wanted to say something.

"Why is it so important to you to find you?" Herbert asked.

"Maybe I'm curious, okay?" Alex snapped back at Herbert. "Maybe I just wanna know how I turned out! Maybe I'm hoping to find a *real partner* to help me protect this city!"

They all stopped and looked at Alex. He looked around. Even he seemed surprised for a second. But only for a second. "Yeah. I said it. 'Cause it's true—neither of you take alien slaying seriously anymore! Herbert's only concerned with his little science experiments, and Sammi's just hanging around waiting for her little pizza and ice cream dream date!"

An entire smoothie splattered against the wall, very close to Alex's head. Sammi walked across the SlayerLair, past Alex, and straight up to Old Man Herbert. She looked angrier than they'd ever seen her.

"Mr. Slewg, if you know anything about what happened to the older version of me, good or bad, please keep it to yourself. I'd rather not know."

She turned and stared daggers at Alex. Then she

walked out of the room.

"Geez," Herbert said. "And I thought I was supposed to be the jerky one."

"*HEY!*" Alex suddenly shot back. "Don't you *ever* talk about her that way, *do you hear me?!*"

"Or else what?"

"Or else I'll pound you in that fat brain of yours, that's what!"

"Without this *fat brain*, you wouldn't even be here!"

"Without that fat brain, *you* wouldn't be here!"

"That makes precisely zero sense!"

"*You* make precisely . . . *negative zero* sense!"

"That is a numeric impossibility!"

"*ENOUGH!*" Old Man Herbert zipped over and floated between them. He took a deep breath to calm himself. "Listen to me. The three of you are like electrons bound to the same nucleus—you're apt to bang against one another now and again. This causes friction. But friction is the source of great energy."

"Spare me the science lecture, old dude," Alex said rudely.

"I'm just saying you're lucky to have each other

as friends, that's all. Take my word for it. I know."

Alex approached Old Man Herbert. "You know a lot of stuff, don't you?" he said, studying the elderly genius. "Like what happened to me."

The 110-year-old scientist glanced over at his younger self, then turned back to face Alex. He took a deep breath. "What happened to you isn't any big secret. In fact, there was a time when you were kind of famous."

Alex's eyes grew wide. He grinned as he plopped into a big squishy chair.

$f(x) = \frac{x}{3} + 5$ $g(x) = 4x^2$

$f(g(x)) = \frac{\{4x^2\}}{3} + 5$

$g(f(x)) = 4\{\frac{x}{3} + 5\}^2$

$h(x) = \begin{cases} 1 & x=2 \\ \frac{3}{x-2} & x \neq 2 \end{cases}$

$A = \pi r^2$

$\left(\frac{6x^4 y^5 z^2}{xy^{-5}z^0}\right)^{-3}$

$\sqrt{25}$ $\sqrt{x^2}$

$\frac{x^2-4}{x+3} \div \frac{x-2}{x^2+5x+6}$

$\sum_{n=0}^{\infty} \left(\frac{1}{2}\right)^n$

$A(t) = A_0(1+\frac{r}{n})^m$

$\pi = 3.14$ _duh!_

$12 \overline{)524} = 43$, 48, 44, 36, 8

1.21 JIGAWATTS

?→ WHAT'S A JIGAWATT?

PARALLEL EVENT PATH

$\left(\frac{\pi}{2}\right)^2 -$

$\frac{1}{2} \times \left(\frac{\pi}{3}\right)^2 -$

$2 \times \frac{1}{2} \times \left(\frac{\pi}{6}\right)^2 =$

$\pi^2/6$

CHAPTER 10

"It's important to understand that my memories aren't the same as yours," old man Herbert said. "The instant you went through the wormhole, you split off from my reality and created a completely different _parallel-event path_."

"Just so you guys know, I'm already confused," Alex said.

"It isn't complicated," Herbert explained. "There are two co-existing versions of our lives. There's the one we live—we were neighbors, blasted through a wormhole, and arrived here."

"And then there's the one I live," Old Man Herbert said. "We were neighbors, we *didn't* find a wormhole, and lived a long, long time to get here."

Alex gave Old Man Herbert a concerned look. "In your version, we weren't . . . *friends or anything*, were we?"

"Far from it. Our mothers forced us to have a playdate together. It was a disaster. We had nothing in common."

"*Whew*," Alex and Herbert sighed together.

"Until we met Sammi."

The two looked at Old Man Herbert.

"We put on the N.E.D. suits I'd invented and went to Alex's backyard to play on his new jungle gym. We found Sammi hiding in the tube slide. She didn't want to go to her swim meet. Alex was embarrassed to be seen in the N.E.D. suit, so we took them off."

"And missed out on discovering the wormhole," Herbert said to Alex. "Way to go, ignoramus."

"It wasn't *me*," Alex said. "It was the umbrella-path version of me."

"*Parallel-event path*," Old Man Herbert corrected him.

"Right. That's what I said." Alex shot a look at young Herbert. "See? Try paying attention."

Old Man Herbert continued. "Alex was eager to come up with fun things to do so Sammi would stay and play with us. I recall he created strange food-related rhyming nicknames. Very odd."

"That doesn't sound like me," Alex said.

"Yes, it does," Herbert shot back.

"So did we spend a lot of time together?" Alex asked. "Sammi and me, I mean."

"No. It was just that one day. The reason I remember it so well is because years later, when all the reporters wanted to know what you were like as a boy, it was the only story I had—a crush on that girl, and food-related rhyming nicknames."

"Reporters asked about Alex?" Herbert asked.

"*Was I famous?!*" Alex asked.

"Yes, you might say that," Old Man Herbert said to both of them. "When I was sixty years old or so, the G'Daliens came down to Earth. They kindly offered to run our planet for us, and allowed the human race to enjoy their vast knowledge and technology. They saved us, and almost everyone loved them."

Old Man Herbert looked directly at Alex. "You'll notice I said '*almost.*'"

"Here we go." Herbert smiled as he settled in.

"I'm confused again," Alex said.

"You—or rather, *my parallel-event-path version of you*—were scared witless of the G'Daliens. And you were *very vocal* about it. You'd rant on and on to anyone who would listen, and many who wouldn't. You were sure the G'Daliens weren't here to help us, but to eat us. You'd talk loudly on buses, give inappropriate toasts at children's birthday parties, and eventually were banned from every karaoke restaurant in Merwinsville."

"But—some of my best friends are G'Daliens," Alex said.

"The media called you 'Fraidy-Cat Filby.' They made fun of you on all the TV shows and in the papers—your paranoid buffoonery was blasted on MonitOrbs all over Merwinsville. As your next-door neighbor, I was constantly interviewed. Everyone wanted to know if you were a strange child growing up. I had to say yes. I mean, rhyming food nicknames? Who does that?"

Herbert was beaming. "This makes perfect sense. When we first came through the wormhole, you were terrified of G'Daliens. You hid behind me, hoping they'd eat me first."

"Interesting," Old Man Herbert said. He studied Alex as if he were in a test tube. "You and Fraidy-Cat Filby had the same fearful tendencies. I'm fascinated with intersecting traits in parallel-event-path selves."

"Okay," Alex snapped angrily. "So what happened to me? Did they lock me up or something?"

"No one knows. After a year of failing to get anyone to join your Anti-G'Dalien League, one day you just went away. Vanished. That was nearly fifty years ago. No one's seen or heard from you since."

Alex got very quiet.

"So . . . the old man version of me could be anywhere. I'll never find myself."

"Hey, you don't have to think about it that way," Herbert offered. "Look on the bright side—maybe you're dead!"

Old Man Herbert watched Alex for a moment. "I probably shouldn't tell you this," he said.

Alex looked up at him. Young Herbert stopped grinning.

"Before you three showed up, before I even knew my parallel self existed, I began having this odd feeling, like there was something I couldn't quite remember. It grew stronger and stronger, until one day I found myself on the rooftop of Andretti's Pizzeria, looking inside an old, rusty air vent. I don't even like pizza. But I knew where my parallel-event-path self—*you, Herbert*—would hide something for me to find. And there it was. My first glimpse into intersecting event paths."

"So . . . you're saying my older self might feel I'm here, and could come and find me?" Alex asked.

"No. I'm saying you might have the power to *find him*. If my theories are correct, I believe you already know where your future self is."

"But—I don't," Alex said.

The older Herbert peered closely at Alex again. "Ask yourself this question: *If you were suddenly alone, betrayed and friendless in this world, where would you go?*"

The more Alex thought about this, the more it made Herbert nervous. "I know what you're thinking, and you can forget it," he said. "You're not running off on a wild Old Man Alex chase to find yourself—you've already got a job protecting the city! You're an AlienSlayer, remember?"

"Who better to find Fraidy-Cat Filby than his parallel-event-path self, AlienSlayer Alex?" Old Man Herbert said excitedly.

"Will you stay out of this?!" Herbert barked at the old man. He turned back to Alex. "Okay. Suppose while you're off wandering around looking for yourself there's an alien attack? What then?"

"Oh, you mean the *tetraquadzillion-to-one* possibility? Strange how suddenly you're so concerned about alien attacks. Of course, you're right—*I'm the only one* who's always on constant lookout! *I'm the only one* who stays vigilant and ready for action! *I'm the only one* everybody cheers the loudest for! You practically admitted it—*I'm the only real AlienSlayer in this whole stinkin' city!*"

"Well, finally we agree on something. You can't just go off looking for yourself. Your expertise at alien slaying is far too important. Maybe you should even consider going solo."

"Fine! Maybe I will go solo! Maybe I'll become,

uh—*SoloSlayer Alex!* No, that's not a good name. But maybe I'll think of a better one! And then maybe I'll get a costume! And maybe I'll be *the greatest AlienSlayer in all the galaxy!*"

"Excuse me, Alex? You asked me to remind you when it was time to go underwear shopping with your mom."

They turned. Chicago stood near the SlayerVator, wearing a bright red, brand-new shirt. EL-ROY was beside him, struggling beneath a pile of what looked like grayish-green rubber.

"It's time. I'm off to do my interview, so EL-ROY will be in charge of today's exit operations."

A tentacle wiggled out and waved. EL-ROY's squeaky, muffled voice came from somewhere under the folds of rubber.

$\mathcal{S}$ lapslapslapslapslapslapslapslapslapslapslap.

The short little G'Dalien's tentacles flapped against the shiny white floor as he crossed the cavernous museum lobby. EL-ROY looked up and down the Hallway of Human History, then turned back and signaled that the coast was clear.

Three oddly floppy-fleshed, grayish-green G'Daliens waddled out from behind a glass-encased Porta-Potty, part of a display called "Humans: Where Did They Go?" Each one's skin seemed way too big for its body, and they had trouble not falling down as they shuffled toward EL-ROY. The last one bounced off a replica of an old wooden outhouse and slammed into the other two.

"Ow! Watch it, you oaf!" whispered one G'Dalien in a muffled voice that sounded remarkably Herbert-like.

"I hate this," muttered a muffled Sammi-ish voice from inside the first baggy blob. "These are the worst disguises *ever.*"

"Shush!" EL-ROY whispered. "Keep your voices down."

The Herbert-sounding baggy-skinned G'Dalien spoke again. "If we're disguised, why do we *also* have to sneak?"

"*Will you two shush it!*" For a little squid, EL-ROY could be pretty bossy. "Okay, move out—*slowly.*"

They all took just a few steps and—*BOING!*—EL-ROY stopped short, causing the others to slam and bounce off each other. The little G'Dalien gave them a threatening look, then peered down the Hallway of Human History. He began waving his tentacles wildly to someone in the distance.

Dallas and Sausalito were waiting at the far end, in front of the caveman diorama, making crazy hand gestures back to EL-ROY.

"Uh-oh," EL-ROY said. "He says we've got company." A group of teenagers were making their way toward the hallway exit. "Stay down. Hopefully this won't get messy."

Herbert flopped his big, green, rubbery butt onto the floor between Alex and Sammi. "I'm surrounded by imbeciles."

Alex and Sammi stood facing each other, awkwardly making eye contact through the mouth holes in their disguises.

"Sorry I threw a smoothie at you," Sammi finally said.

"You should've thrown it at Chicago," Alex said.

"He's just trying to help us."

"How? By getting himself on *Total Universal Inside Access: Merwinsville!* instead of going on a date with you?"

"It wasn't a date!"

"Not to him, obviously. He doesn't like you, y'know. He just likes the AlienSlayer lifestyle."

Sammi shot Alex an angry look, straight through the mouth hole of her rubbery G'Dalien mask. "I don't care if he likes me! I just happen to

77

appreciate what he does for us. You think you don't need *anybody*, that you can do whatever you like, ignore all the rules—"

"*The rules?!* So you're on Herbert's side now? 'Cause you're sounding just as lame and annoying as him!"

"*Excuse me!*" Herbert's voice called out from the floor between them. "I'm sitting right here—I can hear you!"

Alex ignored him and continued arguing with Sammi. "Next thing you're going to say is you agree with Rule Boy that I should just go ahead and become a *solo AlienSlayer!*"

"Well, maybe you should!"

"Maybe I will!"

"Fine!"

"*Fine!*"

The two of them crossed their arms and turned their backs to each other. Herbert stood up, looked at them both, and crossed his arms as well. The three disguised AlienSlayers stood there in their rubbery suits in silence.

Chicago sat on the park bench trying not to look like he was staring. It wasn't easy—the interviewer who'd just wobbled over and sat down next to him was the oddest-looking person he'd ever seen. Her wide, flat face had a thick cake of makeup and enormous dark sunglasses. Her hair was bright yellow and hung down like knotty strands of rope. Even in her large, sacklike, flowery-patterned dress, he could see she was very chubby. When she approached and held out her hand, she nearly tipped over—perhaps because the ends of her thin, tentaclelike legs seemed to be stuffed into a pair of bright red high-heeled shoes.

"I'm so sorry we had to meet in a public park,"

she croaked in a strange, high-pitched lady voice. "Our offices are, um, being sprayed. For rabid space badgers."

"*Total Universal Inside Access: Merwinsville!* has... space badgers?"

"What? Yes! Huge badger problem. Pesky things. We're trying to keep it quiet, so I'm trusting you not to tell anyone."

"Oh, of course. You can count on me."

"*Fabulous*," she oozed. "And hopefully you'll return the favor, and feel free to tell me *any of your secrets.*"

Chicago looked at her, confused for a moment.

"Yes . . . er, *ma'am*."

"Please, call me GOR—uh, GOR-*DONNA*. Now, let's start with the rumors I hear from *very reliable* sources—that the AlienSlayers are *fakes. Frauds. Phonies*."

Chicago didn't expect this. He was one of the very few who knew the AlienSlayers' secret. He thought fast to give her an answer. "The only one I've heard that from is that butt-ugly, ex-janitor G'Dalien who shouts crazy stuff in public."

GOR-DONNA's eye twitched beneath her giant sunglasses. Her chin began to tremble and a strange gurgling sound came out of her throat.

"Oh. I'm sorry," Chicago added quickly, noticing her reaction. "I didn't mean *your* source is that dude. It's just such a crazy thing, and completely untrue, obviously."

"Yes. *Obviously*. Well, I've heard enough. This interview is over. Thank you."

"What? That's it?"

"I'm afraid that we at *T.U.I.A: Merwinsville!* have strict standards as to what we put on our show. We need the juicy stories, the inside scoops no one else knows about. Otherwise, it's not *T.U.I.A:M!* material. Too bad. You could've been on TV."

She heaved her blobby body up off the bench and pretended to straighten her dress as she glanced over at Chicago.

"Wait! I have something *T.U.I.A:M!*-worthy."

"*YES!*" she suddenly growled in an alarmingly deep voice. She cleared her throat. "I mean, how *wonderful*," she added in her lady voice again.

I'M ALL EARS.

EL-ROY watched Dallas swing his arms about wildly.

"Okay. That's the all-clear. Let's move out!"

Alex was still angry. He glared at Sammi and Herbert as they waddled off behind EL-ROY down the hallway. Standing there, he realized the farther they shuffled away from him, the less angry he felt. *What if I did go solo,* he thought. *Maybe I could be the greatest AlienSlayer in all the galaxy.*

Then he looked down at his blobby, ridiculous disguise.

"This is so wrong," he heard himself say. He looked up and spotted the group of teenagers. In an instant, he found himself waddle-running down the hall, chasing after them. He held out a rubbery arm.

"Uh, good day, maties!" He began shouting in the worst Australian accent ever. "You, uh, *bushboogers* enjoying your *little tripsy-doodle* to the museum, thar, *what-what?*"

The teens stared, not sure what to make of him.

"What are you, some kind of G'Dalien pirate?" one teen said.

"Are you feeling all right?" another asked, eyeing his baggy skin suspiciously.

"*I've never felt better,*" Alex said. "Because I am not a pirate . . . or a G'Dalien!" He yanked the rubber mask off his head.

I'M ALEX FILBY—
THE GREATEST ALIENSLAYER
IN THE GALAXY!

The teens were stunned for a moment. But just for a moment.

"It's really him!" one exclaimed. "It's a real AlienSlayer!" Another group heard the call and came running. Soon a mob of museum visitors swarmed Alex. He started laughing as he wriggled out of his bulky costume and scrambled through the growing mob's legs. He began running down the hall, toward the caveman diorama, yelling at the top of his lungs.

"FIRE UP YOUR N.E.D. SUITS! *FIRE UP YOUR N.E.D. SUITS!!*"

Alex's voice echoed down the Hallway of Human History, followed by the screams of the AlienSlayer fans. Dallas and Sausalito saw Alex running toward them, followed by the crazed mob. They stepped up to block them, waving their arms lamely.

"Back! Stay back! Official museum business!"

EL-ROY peeked out from behind the curtain and saw what was coming. *"Not on my watch,"* he muttered. The tiny G'Dalien hopped over the railing and ran toward the oncoming mob. As Dallas and Sausalito let Alex through to the diorama, EL-ROY squeaked to a stop in front of the oncoming teens.

"STOP RIGHT THERE! I ORDER YOU ALL TO IMMEDIATELY—"

FWUMPH!

The mob plowed through EL-ROY's flailing tentacles, sending the mini-squid flying in the air. Dallas and Sausalito struggled to hold back the excited fans as Alex ducked behind the curtain. Sammi and Herbert, out of their G'Dalien costumes and ready to go, stared at him.

"What?" Alex grinned. "Just making my debut."

A dizzy-looking EL-ROY suddenly stumbled through the closed curtain. Using all his tentacles to hold it closed as it was punched and tugged at from the other side, he warily looked up at the three of them.

"Go! Quickly!" he shouted.

Alex, Herbert, and Sammi flipped the switches on the buckles of their N.E.D. suits. In the center of the painted black cave, the shimmering blue light swirled to life.

Alex held his nose as if he were about to dive into a pool. He jumped into the air and cannonballed, solo, into the wormhole.

FOOMP!

Herbert and Sammi shared a look.

FOOMP! FOOMP!

The shimmering blue light vanished and an exhausted EL-ROY slumped over, allowing the curtain to be yanked open. The teens stopped short and stood there in confused silence.

"Take a holo-picture, why don'cha," EL-ROY said. "It'll last longer."

"Please, do go on . . ."

GOR-DONNA's eyes were wide behind her very large, very dark sunglasses. She tried to keep her red lipstick-lined mouth from hanging open as

Chicago finished his story.

"So Alex yells back, 'Maybe I *will* go solo!' I don't think they'd ever break up the AlienSlayer team, of course, but it's a *total universal access* look at *the real people behind the silver suits.* You can use that title if you want."

"Oh, thank you," GOR-DONNA said with a smile. *"Thank you so much."*

"So when will I be on the show?"

"Well, we'll have to verify your main source, of course. I'll need to interview AlienSlayer Alex right away."

"Right. Of course. That makes sense. I'll set it up."

"Excellent," GOR-DONNA said in a deeper, growling voice. She began to laugh in an uncontrollable, not very ladylike manner. *"BWAH-HAH-HAH-HAH-HAH!"*

Chicago looked up from his wristwatch hologram and cut in. "Uh, tomorrow afternoon okay?"

GOR-DONNA stopped laughing. "Yes. That would be fine."

CHAPTER 14

Alex hit the grass at the bottom of the slide, rolled to a stop at his little sister's feet, and grinned up at her.

"Hiya, Ellie-Belly!" he said happily.

"You're in trouble." She held her teddy bear, who was wearing tiny little yellow pajamas. "Mommy's been looking for you."

Alex stood up and smiled at her. "I've just been playing with my friends," he said. As if on cue, Herbert and Sammi popped out of the slide behind him and hit the grass. Ellie eyed all three of them suspiciously.

"There's something weird about your spaceman game," the little girl lisped suspiciously. "I don't like it, Mommy doesn't like it, and Mr. Snugglebuns finds it *highly suspect.*"

She spun around and marched into the house, dragging Mr. Snugglebuns along, his button eye staring at them accusingly.

"*That was a stupid thing you did,*" Herbert snapped at Alex. "Who do you think you are?"

"I'm the greatest AlienSlayer in all the galaxy," Alex said, glancing over at Sammi. "And I do what I want." He turned and walked into his house, leaving Herbert and Sammi standing by the jungle gym.

"Shmoodle-Pie! Try these on—they're adorable!"

Mrs. Filby shoved her arms through the red dressing room curtain and dumped a pile of underpants onto Alex's head. They were banana-yellow, with little smiling monkeys.

"I saw a *darling* set with the days of the week on them so you always know which ones are clean! I'll go get them for you!"

Alex looked at himself in the mirror. Standing

there in his old tighty-whities, he suddenly didn't feel so much like the greatest AlienSlayer in all the galaxy. He didn't even look like the greatest AlienSlayer in all the Merwinsville Mall. He tried puffing his chest out and striking a superhero-y pose.

"That's a little better."

He looked around the tiny dressing room, then reached down and grabbed the bottom of the red curtain. He tied it loosely around his shoulders and grinned. In a single bound, Alex leaped from the heap of underwear onto the dressing room bench.

"Behold! It is I, Alex Filby!"

He stopped. "*Alex Filby*" didn't sound very superhero-y. He thought for a minute.

"It is I, *SoloSlayer Alex*—" Nope. He thought again. His eyes wandered down to the floor, stopping on a set of underwear with different Mexican wrestling characters. Alex cleared his throat, then stood up straight and tall.

"*Behold!* It is I, *EL SOLO LIBRE,* the greatest AlienSlayer in all the galaxy!"

Alex began a series of kung fu/wrestling moves, sparring with his reflection and generally getting all worked up.

"*EL SOLO LIBRE! Lone protector of planets! EL SOLO LIBRE! Enforcer of galactic justice! EL SOLO LIBRE! Butt-kicker of slimy aliens everywhere!*"

He spun around and did a forearm smash-reverse lateral side kick combo off the bench. He landed softly on the pile of underpants, then charged out of the changing room. *POP!* The curtain snapped off the rod. As he bounded through the store, the curtain rings clanged and banged behind him.

"*Alex?*" Mrs. Filby dropped the rainbow of underpants she held in her arms as her son paraded past her wearing nothing but tighty-whities and a dressing room curtain around his shoulders.

"Make way!" Alex bounded past the shop girl folding boxer shorts and out of The Undie Outlet.

Alex got up extra early the next morning and began rummaging through the junk under his bed. His hand felt something slimy. Then something squishy. Then something sticky. Finally, he smiled. He pulled out what he was looking for and held it up—the blue and silver Mexican wrestling mask his Uncle Davey brought him back from Guadalupe.

He pulled the mask over his head and slipped on his N.E.D. suit. Rummaging through the pile of dirty clothes behind his desk, he found a damp, striped beach towel. He gave it a sniff—a little mildewy, but not too stinky. He tied it around his shoulders and stood in front of the full-length mirror on the back of his bedroom door.

Knock knock!

"Doodlebug? Are you up?"

Alex leaped back to his bed and dove under the covers. He pulled them up to his neck and said, "C'mon in, Mom!"

His mother opened the door. She gave her son an odd look, shut her eyes tightly, and took a deep breath.

"Alex, this isn't easy," she said in a serious tone.

"But your father and I have decided—"

"*WOO-HOO! I BEAT THE LEACACOSIANS! EAT BLASTER DUST, YOU FILTHY SPACE-WORMS!*" Mr. Filby's strained voice echoed from downstairs. Alex's mom shut her eyes tightly again and continued.

"*I have decided,* in light of yesterday's display at the mall, that you need to partake in more traditionally *normal* activities. I've signed you up for sleepover camp this weekend. After today, no more spaceman game. It's for your own good."

"*What?!* Mom, you can't do that! Listen, I know I was acting a little weird at The Undie Outlet, but there's no need for you to worry—it's completely out of my system, I swear!"

She gave him another odd look. "Uh-huh. Somehow, sweetie, I don't find you very convincing right now." She walked out, shutting the door behind her. Alex stared at his reflection in the full-length mirror on the back of the door.

He was still wearing the blue and silver Mexican wrestling mask his Uncle Davey had brought back from Guadalupe.

CHAPTER 15

$\mathbb{S}$pecial Agent Illinois scanned the mass of Merwinsvillians gathered outside the entrance to the Flee-a-seum. Satisfied it was safe, he nodded to Mayor CROM-WELL. The mayor stepped to the front of the TransPodium and greeted the crowd. There were as many Merwinsvillians as the day before, and they cheered loudly as the mayor pulled out a large, golden pair of scissors.

"Ugh. *Again* with the giant gold props?"

Slumped between Herbert and Sammi near the back of the TransPodium, Alex wasn't happy. He could only think about how this might be his last day in Future Merwinsville, at least for a while. If his mother stuck to her decision (and she always did, especially the ones for his own good), by this time tomorrow he'd most likely be setting up a tent in the park four blocks from his house.

The mayor gestured for the three of them to come forward and do the honors of letting the crowd enter the Flee-a-seum.

Herbert and Sammi stepped up and took the giant scissors.

"C'mon, Alex!" Sammi said.

"Quit moping," Herbert added. "You can cut the ribbon, okay?"

Alex looked at the two of them holding the stupid giant scissors. A question popped into his head: *Is this how El Solo Libre would spend his last day in Future Merwinsville?*

The answer, he realized, was no.

"No thanks," he said. "I've got some stuff to do." Alex stepped to the back edge of the TransPodium and looked down. Its back end hovered over the vast, empty Flee-a-seum field on the other side of the ribbon.

Alex looked back and smiled at Herbert and Sammi. He held his nose and cannonballed off the TransPodium.

"I'm really starting to hate it when he does that," Herbert said.

Alex hit the ground, rolled to a stop, and smiled as he looked across the empty field. If this was his last day in Future Merwinsville, he was gonna make the best of it. He started walking toward the exit at the far end of the field—then heard something that stopped him in his tracks.

"*Five! Four! Three! . . .*" Oh, no. The mayor was leading the crowd in a countdown. Alex suddenly realized he'd made a big mistake.

"*. . . Two! One! WELCOME!*"

The crowd's roar boomed and bounced off the empty stadium seats. A half second later the entire population of Merwinsville flooded onto the Flee-a-seum field—and were charging right at Alex.

Alex began to run for the exit and made it halfway across the field when he tripped. The crowd was like a tidal wave about to wash him away. Trapped, he stood up and looked back at them. *Perfect*, he thought. So this is how he'd spend his last day—

drowning in his fans.

BONK! Something hard hit him in the head. "And they're throwing things at me?" he said.

Looking up, he saw that what hit him was the bottom rung of a rope ladder, which was attached to a sleek AirCar hovering overhead. Chicago waved down to him.

"Grab it!" Chicago yelled. "Quickly!"

Alex grabbed it and immediately began to rise above the crowd. As the mob reached the center of the circular field, a few jumped up and grabbed his leg and hung off him. Alex shook them loose and watched them drop safely to the field below.

Chicago circled skyward as Alex hung on, swinging widely over the Flee-a-seum field, which was now swarming with Merwinsvillians.

"*Yeeeehaawww!*"

Alex climbed up and hopped into the mayor's shiny SkyLimo. He grinned at Chicago, then noticed the very large, rather strange-looking woman sitting behind him.

"Alex, this is *GOR-DONNA*, from *Total Universal Inside Access: Merwinsville!* I told her all about you, and she wants to interview you! How awesome is that?"

GOR-DONNA extended a flabby arm and shook Alex's hand. "From what I can tell, you're the one *true* AlienSlayer. I'd love to get *your* story."

Alex studied her for a moment, then turned to Chicago. "Okay. But I'm driving."

"What?"

"You heard me, Chi-town! Move it on over!"

Chicago slid over and Alex jumped behind the controls. "Okay, where do you wanna do this thing?"

"How about *the SlayerLair?*" GOR-DONNA said quickly.

"Sounds like a plan! First round of Mega-Choco-Bomb Rootbeer Marshmallow Smoothies on me!"

Alex gunned the ship and it zoomed across the sky, nearly smashing into a MonitOrb floating over Main Street.

As the citizens of Merwinsville explored their new Flee-a-seum, Mayor CROM-WELL led Sammi and Herbert away from the crowd to an enormous oblong-shaped building at the opposite end of the stadium. Inside, a mountain of brownish rubber was being slowly inflated by an enormous, heavy-looking machine. It had the silver-plated words *INFLATATRON 3000* on the side, and made a disturbing metallic wheezing sound as it worked to pump air into the massive pile of floppy material.

"What is that thing?" Sammi asked.

"It's an InflataTron," Herbert said. "Duh."

"No, I mean what's it *inflating*?"

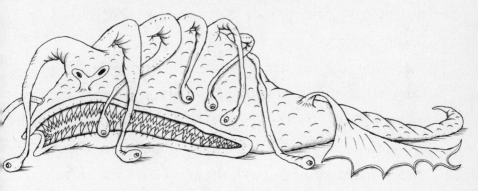

Mayor CROM-WELL stepped up and gestured grandly. "It's a balloon replica of a Klapthorian Winged Death Slug! An integral part of our Flee-a-bration, designed to provide a lifelike source of terror for our historical Flee-enactment! Fully inflated, it will be terrifyingly life-size!"

"Well," Herbert observed. "Can't have a parade without a good parade floatie."

Sammi looked at the pile of mushy brown rubber. "It reminds me of those ridiculous G'Dalien costumes we wear when we sneak—"

"A*hem!*" Herbert cut her off, glaring at her. Her eyes widened, surprised that she'd almost blown their secret in front of the mayor, of all non-people.

"Oops, sorry. Never mind."

Luckily the mayor was busy describing the horror his giant parade balloon represented and hadn't noticed Sammi's slipup.

"The Klapthorians raise these beasts by feeding them whatever they pillage from other planets, like our precious LUNN-CHMUNNY." His blobby belly wiggled as he shuddered with the memory. "They fatten them up and make them mean, then travel with them from galaxy to galaxy, stealing more and feeding them more and stealing more and feeding them more and—"

"We grasp the pattern," Herbert interjected.

"Gosh," Sammi said. "Thank goodness this is just a blow-up doll. I'd hate to have to meet a real one face-to-face."

Herbert glared at her again. The mayor had stopped talking. Herbert quickly flashed him a reassuring smile.

"Er, not that we couldn't handle the job. After all, we *are* AlienSlayers, *remember?*"

"Oh. Right," Sammi answered. "We sure are!"

She excused herself to get some air and walked outside.

LO-PEZ was busy finishing off a bucket of Kelgarian Fried Chorple wings at his post outside the front entrance of the SlayerLair when he looked up. A shiny object was getting larger as it zoomed straight toward him. He dropped his bucket and heaved his heavy body into a shrubbery just as the SkyLimo nearly crash-landed onto the sidewalk. Alex pulled up at the last second and jerked it to a stop.

He hopped out and slapped LO-PEZ on the belly. "Hiya, L. P.!"

"I'll, uh, just leave you two, then," Chicago said weakly. He opened the door to let GOR-DONNA out. Chicago got back into the driver's seat and lifted away very, very slowly.

GOR-DONNA stumbled in her high heels toward Alex, who was waiting by the SlayerVator. As she passed LO-PEZ, the G'Dalien doorman quickly wiped Chorple grease off his face with a tentacle, sucked in his massive gut, and spoke in an odd, deep, cheesy-sounding voice. "Well. G'Day to you, *m'lady*."

GOR-DONNA growled at the grinning LO-PEZ as she passed him and got on the SlayerVator. The doors slid shut and LO-PEZ sighed, letting his sucked-in gut flop out again. "Now *that's* what I call a woman."

"Root beer. Fudge brownies. Oreo cookies. Marshmallows. And keep 'em comin'!" Alex smiled as the auto smoothie bar produced two of his famous Mega-Choco-Bomb Marshmallow Root Beer Smoothies. He took one for himself and slid the other across the bar to GOR-DONNA.

"Ooh, thank you," she said with a smile. She took a big slurp and immediately gagged as she tried to swallow the syrupy-thick brown-sugar-liquid. "What a lovely lair you have here," she choked.

"Yeah. It's okay."

SLURP! Alex took a big swig of his smoothie.

"Okay. Ask me anything. I'm feeling loose."

She pulled a glossy photograph and a black marker from her purse and shoved them in his face.

"First of all, I'm a big fan—of *yours*."

Alex looked down at the photo. The picture was of him, Herbert, and Sammi. Herbert and Sammi's faces were scribbled over in crayon, and scrawled above them were very rude and inappropriate comments.

Alex shrugged, signed the photograph, and handed it back to his new giant-headed lady fan. She took the picture and beamed at it before stuffing it back into her purse.

"Nothing personal against your *little friends*," she said. "It's just that I can tell you're the *real* AlienSlayer. The other two don't share your *natural greatness*, if you know what I mean."

Alex smiled a bit. "Yeah," he said. "I kinda do."

"So my question is, have you ever thought of going *solo*?"

Alex stared at his interviewer. "Whoa. You're good."

Chicago flew straight back to the Flee-a-seum and picked up Sammi and Herbert. He couldn't wait to share the news that *he* was going to be on *Total Universal Inside Access: Merwinsville!* As he drove them to Andretti's Pizzeria, talking about himself the entire way, Sammi grew more and more uncomfortable.

"I mean, I think it went very well," he blabbed on. "I'm not saying I'll be more famous than you guys, of course, but if I get on TV and people like me, who knows? Maybe I could be, like, the official on-air spokesperson for, y'know, stuff."

Herbert and Sammi shared a quick look. Sammi was eager to change the subject. "You sure it's okay for you to be cruising around in Mayor CROM-WELL's SkyLimo?"

"I was on official AlienSlayer business, so it's cool. Hey, do you think I should've worn a blue shirt? Red felt like a good call, but you're a girl. I probably should've asked you."

"What AlienSlayer business?" Herbert cut in. "We were at the event—with the mayor."

"Not all of you." Chicago veered the AirCar toward the old brick pizza building below. "I got Alex a *solo interview* with the top reporter at *T.U.I.A:M!* She and I are pretty tight now."

"Ah," Herbert said. "How perfect."

Chicago made a soft landing in front of Andretti's Pizzeria. Herbert jumped out. Sammi waited for Chicago to get out and maybe open her door, but he didn't even unbuckle himself.

"Aren't you coming in?" she asked.

"Can't. The reporter said I might be on TV. I've gotta be ready. I'm gonna get a haircut, manicure, maybe buy some new clothes. I've gotta be on my game, in case I get the call."

Herbert rolled his eyes. "I'll go get a booth—for two."

Sammi studied Chicago's grinning face. Then she got an idea. "Hey," she said carefully. "What would you think if Herbert, Alex, and I decided to tell everyone that we're not really AlienSlayers?"

Chicago froze. He looked at her, dumbfounded. Then he forced a chuckle. "Heh. Uh, why would you wanna do that?"

"'Cause it's the truth?"

"I know, but you'd lose the fame, the love of the people—"

"The mayor's car."

Chicago glanced at her and squirmed nervously in his seat. "You wouldn't get any press coverage as normal, boring kids. Who'd want to talk to you?"

Sammi opened the door and stepped out of the SkyLimo. "My *friends*, that's who."

"El Solo Libre. I like the sound of that." GORDONNA stared at a grinning Alex, who was into his fifth Mega-Choco-Bomb Marshmallow Root Beer Smoothie.

He nodded slowly. "I know. Awesome, right?"

"So how would El Solo Libre be any different from AlienSlayer Alex? Or Herbert? Or Sammi?"

"*Pfff.* Please. *Much* cooler costume, for one thing. And he wouldn't show aliens any mercy. He would show them some pretty devastating kung fu/Mexican wrestling combo moves, though. Which would be *devastating.* If you were an alien, I mean."

"I see. And what if he came face to face with a Klapthorian DeathSlug?"

"You mean those things that scared away all the G'Daliens all those years ago? Well, first of all, no *way* would El Solo Libre just run away and give up without a fight. He'd get up in their faces and be all, '*Yeah?! You want summa this? Huh? HUH?*' That'd probably be enough to scare 'em. Wouldn't even have to lift a finger."

SLUUURRRRP!

Alex finished off another smoothie. He was feeling good. He noticed his interviewer smiling at him. An even wider grin came over her enormous face.

"What?"

She leaned in close and spoke in a hushed voice. "I probably shouldn't tell you this, but as an intergalactic

reporter, I have the contact information of a wide variety of life-forms throughout the universe—*both friendly and unfriendly.*"

"I'm listening."

"It might be good for the story to see *firsthand* how a *solo AlienSlayer* would talk to a race of notorious space bullies."

Alex's eyes grew wide. He began imagining tough-sounding things he might say to some slimy alien a zillion miles away.

"Oh, but what was I thinking? In order to make an intergalactic alien call, we'd need access to some kind of powerful, high-tech, top-of-the-line supercomputer—"

"Hey!" Alex exclaimed. *"We've got one of those!"*

GOR-DONNA suddenly looked over at the

massive SarcasmaTron. It nearly ran from one end of the lair to the other.

"What an extraordinary coincidence! So you do!"

Alex was suddenly struck with a pang of *sheer wrongness*—using the SlayerLair supercomputer to crank call a race of mean and violent space bullies was highly irresponsible, potentially dangerous, and 100 percent guaranteed to make Herbert and Sammi really, *really* angry.

"Let's do it," he said.

Herbert sat waiting at a table near the door of Andretti's Pizzeria, staring down at his favorite combo: spinach, olives, and mushrooms, with extra anchovies. He took advantage of the fact that his booth was the only one not violently flying around the antigravity restaurant and slowly lifted a fat, greasy slice to his mouth.

CRASH! SPLAT! The slice went flying out of his hand and stuck to the nearby wall as a flying booth slammed into his.

CLICK! A G'Dalien took his picture with a tiny camera. "G'Day!" She giggled, waving excitedly. "Huge fan!"

Herbert tightened his seatbelt and reached for another slice of his smelly pizza.

Sammi suddenly jumped into the seat next to him, causing him to drop the slice in his lap. She looked upset as she buckled up.

As Herbert tried again, Sammi gripped the wheel in the center of the table and spun it around. Their booth veered off into the center of the restaurant, joining the others in a crazy, dangerous dance. As she angrily whirled their booth faster and faster, they bounced around the room, and she started to feel better.

SMASH! SPLORT!

Another slice flew out of Herbert's hand and landed in the birthday cake of a little girl who was zooming by.

Herbert hated this place.

"I'm officially calling a team meeting."

"We can't. Alex isn't here."

"Which is fortunate, since he's the topic of our team meeting. Alex has recently displayed a dangerously independent streak. And I'm beginning to observe signs of behavioral abnormalities in you as well."

"*Behavioral abnormalities?*" Sammi spun the wheel. Herbert's side of the table crashed into a booth full of Anti-Gravi-T-Ball players, dousing him in fruit juice.

"Between you forgetting yourself in front of the mayor and Alex walking away from a huge public event to do a one-on-one interview, I feel it's time we reviewed The Rules."

"Or maybe it's time we just told everyone the truth." Sammi ducked to avoid a piping-hot slice of pepperoni as it sailed by her head and smacked Herbert in the face.

He peeled it off. "We've discussed this already. It doesn't do anyone any good to tell, and it isn't doing anyone any harm to not tell. End of discussion."

"I don't know about that anymore," Sammi said. "This whole Flee-Festival nonsense, celebrating how the G'Daliens allowed themselves to be kicked off their home planet by a bunch of bullies. It's pathetic! They've never stood up for themselves, and now that we've tricked them into thinking we'll fight their battles for them, they never will."

Herbert sighed. "*Again*, the chances of an alien attack are a *tetraquadzillion*-to-one. It's a virtual impossibility that we'll ever have to do anything even remotely heroic."

Sammi spun the wheel again, this time slamming the booth to a stop. She unbuckled and turned to Herbert.

"The fact that we don't *have to do anything* to get all of this fame and SkyLimos and stuff is exactly what bothers me. And I know if we told Alex the truth, it'd bother him, too. So that makes you and Chicago the only ones who don't mind being total and complete phonies. It doesn't take a genius to see who's behaving abnormally around here."

Sammi turned and stormed out of Andretti's. Herbert watched her, then suddenly realized his booth wasn't moving. He smiled down at his food.

"Finally," he said, carefully lifting his last slice of spinach, olives, and mushrooms with extra anchovies pizza.

KERRRRASH! A pizza booth carrying a beefy G'Dalien family slammed into him, smushing the smelly slice all over his face.

GOR-DONNA entered data into SarcasmaTron at lightning speed. She and Alex were surrounded by a dozen empty Mega-Choco-Bomb Root Beer Marshmallow Smoothie mugs.

"*BROOOOOAAAARRRRRP!*"

GOR-DONNA's massive belch didn't slow down her tapping.

"My, you *are* a charming beauty, aren't you?" the sassy supercomputer quipped.

"SarcasmaTron!" Alex said. "GOR-DONNA is our guest. And besides that, she's a lady."

"Of course she is. And I'm a toaster oven."

GOR-DONNA hit another button. The HoloScreen on SarcasmaTron came to life. "Okay," she said. "Contact with Klapthorian operator base established. Let's hope they pick up."

Alex put on his game face as the transmission began to crackle and pop. "This is gonna be *so cool*," he whispered.

KRRGGT . . . KRRGGT . . . FZZZZT! SarcasmaTron's HoloScreen projection rippled, cutting in and out for a few seconds.

Then it appeared.

Floating in the center of the room was the head of a Klapthorian. The hideous creature's flesh had the color and texture of a chunk of meatloaf left out in the sun a few million years too long. Popping out 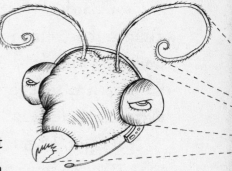 on either side of its stubbly, antennaed head were a pair of bulging, bright-yellow eyes with no eyelids. Its unblinking glare gave it a disturbed, angry look. Alex's first thought was that he would *not* want to get into a staring contest with this nasty bug monster.

Its jagged beak suddenly snapped open, and the horrible creature spoke.

"*Mmm, y'ello?*"

"Yeah. You a Klapthorian?"

"Last time I checked!" the horrid creature tittered pleasantly. "And with whom am I speaking, please?"

"I'll tell you *whom* you're speaking with. The greatest AlienSlayer in all the galaxy, that's who—EL SOLO LIBRE!"

"And how may I help you today, Mr. Libre?"

"You don't help me. I help *you*. By changing my mind and deciding *not* to kick your butt. Which I *won't*. So forget it!"

Alex had to fight the urge to burst into an overexcited giggle fit.

"All right, let me just read back your message to you. You've come to the decision to change your mind and do a favor by opting *against* any butt-kicking. Do I have that right, Mr. Libre?"

"Wait. *What?* No, no! I said I won't *change my mind* about *not* kicking your butt, meaning I will be kicking—"

"I'm sorry. How may I direct your call?"

"Oh. You're not the leader of the Klapthorians?"

"Ah. Please hold. I'm connecting you now."

Soft Muzak played.

Alex glanced over at GOR-DONNA. "Try being more direct," she suggested. "Maybe get to it a little quicker." Alex nodded. A new Klapthorian face appeared, uglier and meaner than the last one.

"Who is this?"

"El Solo Libre," Alex said, a little less sure of himself.

"Okay. State your business."

"Uh, kicking your butt . . . ?"

The creature stared with unblinking eyes for a moment. His beak twisted upward into a tiny grin. *"Franglaxx?"* He laughed. "You crazy son-of-a-quasar, is that you?"

"No! This is EL SOLO LIBRE! The greatest AlienSlayer in all the galaxy, and sole protector of the G'Daliens!"

"Sorry. The Ga-*Dealios?*"

"G'Daliens! The alien race you bullied into fleeing from their home planet, like, fifty years ago! Ring any bells?"

"Fifty years?! D'you know how many alien races we bully? I can't remember whose planet we invaded fifty *minutes* ago."

"Well, you invaded the wrong one on that fateful day, *space shrimp*. You stole my friends' LUNN-CHMUNNY, and now it's payback time—*El Solo Libre*–style."

There was a long silence. The Klapthorian leader's stubby little antennae twitched. He spoke slowly and directly.

"What did you say?"

"I said a bunch of stuff. You really want me to repeat it all? Let's see, I mentioned LUNN-CHMUNNY, said 'it's payback time,' ended with 'El Solo Libre–style . . .'"

"No, before all that. You called me . . . *a name*."

"Oh, right. Stinkbug? No . . . was it dung beetle?"

GOR-DONNA leaned in. "I believe he said, '*space shrimp*.'"

"*THAT'S IT!*" The Klapthorian leader suddenly shrieked. "NO ONE REFERS TO THE KLAPTHORIAN RACE AS SHRIMP! WE ARE ALL-POWERFUL! YOU AND YOUR PLANET SHALL BE DESTROYED!"

"Now we're getting somewhere," Alex said. "Why

don't you come down here to Earth and just *try* to destroy us, *shrimp-ola!*"

"CHALLENGE ACCEPTED! YOU WILL BE ANNIHILATED! PLEASE HOLD!"

The leader slammed its clawlike pincer on a console. Alex was face-to-face again with the nice Klapthorian receptionist.

"Okie-dokie, let's see here. The earliest availability I have for a global annihilation would be this Saturday, sometime between noon and four. We'll see you then. Have a terrific day!"

FZZZZT! The Klapthorian disappeared, and the HoloScreen went blank. Alex blinked. Suddenly his tummy hurt. He also had a throbbing ice cream headache.

"*Saturday?*" he murmured to himself. "But I'll be *camping.*"

"BWA-*HWAAHWAAHWAA!*" The sudden, disturbing laugh stopped Alex cold. He spun around to see his guest jumping up and down excitedly inside the SlayerVator.

"REVENGE SHALL BE MINE!" GOR-DONNA growled in a strangely lower-sounding voice. "*SEE YA SATURDAY, SOLO SUCKER!*"

The doors closed, leaving Alex sitting alone with his thoughts, his tummy ache, and a very sarcastic supercomputer.

"Well," SarcasmaTron said. "She seemed nice."

chapter 19

Sammi and Herbert entered the SlayerLair to find Alex sitting in a squishy chair, rubbing his belly. She eyed the empty smoothie mugs cluttered all over the floor.

"What happened here?" she asked.

"And what's with all these empties?" Herbert added. "Did you drink all of these yourself?"

"I don't wanna talk about it," Alex replied, careful not to look either of them in the eye. "I just got a little thirsty."

"A *little*? You should have your stomach pumped!"

"Yeah. I need to lie down. I don't feel too well."

They both eyed Alex suspiciously.

"In his defense, some of those are mine," SarcasmaTron wisecracked.

Chicago entered with an armful of rubber G'Dalien suits. "Sorry, guys, it's time," he said in a sad tone. "EL-ROY's gonna have to lead you out again—my Dad's making me wash and wax the mayor's SkyLimo." He looked right at Alex. "*Someone got it all scratched up.*"

GOR-DON was still chuckling fiendishly to himself as he slunk through the back alley behind City Hall. As he made his way he yanked the yellow wig off the top of his head and kicked the high-heeled shoes off the two tentacles he used as human legs.

"I don't know *how* they wear those things."

"*Gordy?*"

The giant G'Dalien spun around to face an almost equally large *actual* woman standing on the sidewalk. Her curly hair was pulled back in a hairnet and she had a puzzled look on her chubby face. It was the same woman from his framed photograph. She stared at his makeup.

GOR-DON straightened up to make himself look taller. "Hello, Marion," he said. "You're looking well."

She looked at his frilly dress. "What are you *wearing?*"

"This old thing?"

Marion suddenly smiled warmly. "Oh, I get it! It's your costume for the Great G'Dalien Flee-Festival this Saturday! What a wonderful tribute to your human hosts! I love it!"

Marion flashed him her T-shirt. It read: *I ♥ ALIENSLAYERS!*

"What are *you wearing?!*" GOR-DON exclaimed.

"I'm volunteering to help with the event—and I'm hoping *they'll* be there so I can meet them!"

GOR-DON's evil glee quickly turned sour. His eyes welled up, smudging his makeup.

"Your, uh—mascara is running," Marion noticed.

"How could you?" He began, almost in a whisper.

"Oh, it shouldn't be too hard," she said. "I'll just help people find their seats, pass out banners and flags, maybe lead the crowd in a few cheers—*Gimme an A! Gimme an L! Gimme an—*"

"I don't mean how could you help," he suddenly snapped. "I mean, how could you be a *fan* of those—*pseudo-slayer scum?!*"

She gasped and stared at him. He took a deep breath and wiped his face with a tentacle, smearing his makeup across his quivering cheeks.

"All right, Marion. Believe in your *precious AlienSlayers* for just a little longer. But here—you're going to want to keep this."

He handed her a small business card. She stared at it.

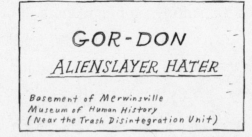

GOR-DON

ALIENSLAYER HATER

Basement of Merwinsville
Museum of Human History
(Near the Trash Disintegration Unit)

"Yep, I got my own place now. Moved out of Mom's guesthouse, just like you suggested. Well, technically she kicked me out after I lost my job as head janitor because my evil plot for complete domination by causing chaos and unrest between humans and G'Daliens was foiled by your little friends there."

Marion nodded carefully and slowly stepped away from him as he continued. "But I've got another plan in place, so you should stop by. We'll catch up, talk about old times, await the destruction of the city, and emerge from the rubble to enslave any survivors. I'll make you that chicken curry you like. With the peas."

She pocketed the card and continued to back away.

"Seriously, don't lose that card. Because the day is soon coming when your so-called AlienSlayers will face a real challenger, and they'll be exposed as the *WORTHLESS, LYING FAKERS* they are! Then you'll see! *You'll all see! BWAH-HAH-HAH-HAH!!!*"

GOR-DON's insane laughter echoed off the alley walls for a good long while, until he finally stopped and noticed Marion was gone. He looked around. She was across the street, running away from him as fast as she could.

"She'll be back."

Alex, Herbert, and Sammi sat silently in the backseat of the Slewg family station wagon for the entire ride to the Merwinsville Mall. When Herbert's mom pulled up to the curb, she turned around to face them.

"All right. I want all three of you to march straight to the food court, order your favorite junky food, sit down together, and *talk out whatever's going on between you.* Got it?"

Herbert rolled his eyes.

Alex stared out the window.

Sammi said, "Thanks for the ride, Mrs. Slewg."

The three of them piled out and walked toward the entrance as a group of eighth-grade girls were coming out. Mrs. Slewg honked her horn. Everyone looked up as she stuck her head out and shouted from the car window.

"And Herbie, remember—you're lactose intolerant! No dairy, or you'll have the rootsy-tooters all night, okay, sweetie?!"

The girls laughed. Herbie dropped his head and walked into the mall.

At the food court, Sammi got a chicken chimichanga with extra hot sauce. Herbert got a plain burger with no bun and extra anchovies on the side. Alex got a SuperCheezyFrankOnnaStick, with an extra stick.

The three of them sat down and began to eat in silence. Finally Sammi spoke up.

"Somebody say something! I'm sick of fighting."

Alex and Herbert traded looks.

"All right, I'll begin," Herbert said. "I don't think either of you, but especially Alex, have been respectful of the pre-agreed Rules and Terms we all pre-agreed to."

"Well, that's an easy one to solve," Alex snapped. "My mom's making me go to sleepaway camp this weekend, so I won't be going through the wormhole at all for a while. So you and your stupid pre-agreed terms can have fun in the future together!"

"See?" Herbert said to Sammi. "He called the pre-agreed terms 'stupid.' This is what I'm talking about. This is the problem."

"All right, all right," Sammi said. "Your mom's really doing that?"

Alex nodded. "She says no more playing 'space-man' with you guys—thinks it's abnormal."

"If only she knew," Herbert said.

"Well," Sammi said, "I guess that means none of us go through this weekend, and then we'll just have to see. Maybe it's time we took a break, anyway."

WHAT?

Herbert and Alex spat out a sardine and a hunk of hot dog, respectively.

"We've been going every day for months! We can't *all* just suddenly take a *weekend off*!" Alex said.

"Alex is right!" Herbert exclaimed. The two boys looked at each other. This was a first. It even *sounded* awkward. "More important, I've got some work I was hoping to finish up in the lab."

"It's your rule," Sammi said. "Either we all go through together, or no one does, remember?"

"Well, technically it was more of a guideline than a rule," Herbert said.

"I completely agree with Herbert," Alex said. They looked at each other again (this was starting to get creepy).

Alex's mind was racing. *Someone* had to fight the Klapthorians, and Herbert and Sammi were the only ones even remotely qualified. Besides, he thought, defeating this alien menace just might remind the two of them of the importance of being AlienSlayers. "Seriously, you guys. Just because I can't go this weekend doesn't mean you shouldn't. You should. Especially on Saturday, from like noon to four."

"Do I get a vote?" Sammi asked. "Because I think this weekend is the perfect time to take a break. This big Flee-Festival thing is all about running away from aliens. Not exactly an AlienSlayer-approved message. I say we stay home."

Herbert took a bite of his anchovy burger. Alex saw he was backing down. It was bad enough that he'd special-ordered a Klapthorian attack for the big day, and that he couldn't be there to help protect Merwinsville; now, because of him, the city would be completely without any AlienSlayers at all.

"I don't like this, guys," he blurted nervously. "What if—what if Saturday's *the day*?"

"What day?" Herbert said.

"The day there's finally another alien attack!"

"Oh, Alex," Sammi said.

Herbert rolled his eyes.

"What?" Alex exclaimed. "Look, I know the *tetraquadzillion-to-one* factor, but the 'one' in that means there's still *one chance* there could be an attack! And if there is, Merwinsville is gonna need you two to do your jobs!"

"There won't be an attack," Sammi said. "And even if there were, and all three of us could be there—there'd be nothing we could do to stop it."

"What are you talking about?" Alex looked at Herbert. "What is she talking about?"

Sammi and Herbert shared a look. "It's time," she said.

"Time for what?" Alex asked.

Herbert nodded to Sammi. Then he looked at Alex. "Time to go to the arcade."

Herbert led Alex and Sammi past rows and rows of kids standing in front of arcade video games, tapping, jumping, shooting, and blasting.

"I just don't see the point of these things," Alex said.

"You used to," Herbert said, pointing up at the wall.

"Wow, who knew there was another Alex Filby in the metropolitan Merwinsville area?"

Sammi put a hand on his shoulder. "There isn't, Alex."

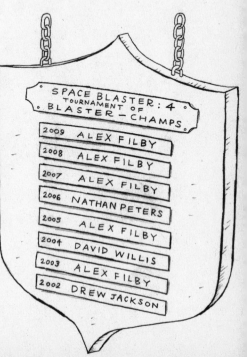

SPACE BLASTER: 4
TOURNAMENT OF
BLASTER — CHAMPS

2009	ALEX FILBY
2008	ALEX FILBY
2007	ALEX FILBY
2006	NATHAN PETERS
2005	ALEX FILBY
2004	DAVID WILLIS
2003	ALEX FILBY
2002	DREW JACKSON

Herbert stopped at a large, interactive arcade version of the game AlienSlayer: 3-D! Standing in its stall-like box, facing its big screen, was a six-year-old kid with shaggy hair. He was wearing giant mittens and holding a large plastic staff. He stood in a ready stance, waiting for the next challenge.

There's something weirdly familiar about this, Alex thought.

The kid crouched in front of the screen as the game announced, "PEOPLE OF EARTH! PREPARE TO BE INVADED BY ALIENS!" All at once, an army of holographic reptilian creatures began to hop out of the screen.

The little boy chopped wildly at his 3-D attackers, swinging the staff, taking them on and cutting them down one by one.

Alex's eyes suddenly grew wide.

"Hey! Check it out! They made a video game of our victory!"

"Alex—"

Alex cut Sammi off as he stepped up beside the little boy. "Okay, kid. You're gonna want to use your staff here. Trust me—I know what's coming."

The kid gave Alex a look. "So do I, dorkface. I have the high score. Now back off and stop trying to play my game for me."

"I don't need to play it, kid. *I lived it.*"

Alex stepped out and smiled at Herbert and Sammi. They weren't smiling back.

"A video game of our *exact battle*?! I knew we were famous, but I didn't know we were *that famous.* They must've gathered all the heroic details from the future, then come back to the present and designed the—"

He stopped, suddenly confused. "Wait a minute. If that happened in the *future,* then how'd they—"

Sammi put a hand on his shoulder. "Oh, Alex. I'm so sorry."

At the food court, Alex paced back and forth in front of the SuperCheezyFrankOnnaStick stall.

"We're fakes?! Why didn't you tell me?!"

He held six of the goopy, pierced wieners in his two hands, and Herbert was at the counter ordering him more. He stuffed another SuperCheezyFrankOnnaStick into his mouth.

"Slow down on those things," Sammi said.

"Sorry," he said coldly. "I tend to overeat when I've been *totally betrayed by my friends.*" He kept on pacing. "So, we don't have *any* alien slaying skills?!"

"I'm afraid not. We're just . . . normal, boring *kids.*"

Alex stopped pacing and looked Sammi in the eye. "All this time—I can't believe you lied to me."

Sammi turned away. She felt horrible.

"Oh, stop it, already." Herbert walked over with three more dogs, sniffing them with scientific curiosity. "There was no harm done, and you got to believe you were a real live superhero, just as every man, woman, child, and G'Dalien living in Future

Merwinsville still believes. A belief, by the way, that I vote we allow to continue."

Sammi shot him a stern look. Herbert nodded. "We'll discuss that later. The main thing to remember is that no one was ever in danger. The chances of an actual alien attack taking place are a tetraquadzillion-to—"

PLOP!

Alex's SuperCheezyFrankOnnaStick hit the floor with a splatter. Herbert and Sammi stared at him. He looked frozen, like he was in shock.

"Alex?" Sammi asked gently.

"Oh, no," he said. "What have I done . . ."

He turned and focused on Herbert and Sammi's confused expressions. He wanted to tell them but knew they couldn't help him anymore. They were just normal, boring kids now.

There's only one person who can help me now, he thought to himself. *El Solo Libre*.

"Alex, you're making me nervous," Sammi said. "What is it?"

He shook his head. "I gotta go." He took one last look at Herbert and Sammi, then Alex ran out of the food court.

Alex hit the cool, moonlit Merwinsville night air and stopped. He stood in the middle of the mall parking lot and looked up for any signs of Klapthorian Death Cruisers, then remembered the attack wasn't due for another hundred years. He thought of Herbert and Sammi and felt angry, but also lonely and confused, like he didn't know exactly who he was.

How could they do this?

Staring up at the full moon, Alex wished he

could go somewhere and · just disappear. Then he remembered something Old Man Herbert had said:

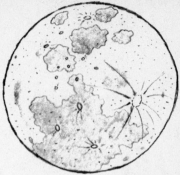

"*If you were suddenly alone, betrayed and friendless in this world, where would you go?*"

Suddenly, Alex realized what he had to do. He ran all the way home without stopping once—the bright, full moon lighting his way.

The next morning, Alex jumped out of bed and tripped over a mound of dirty clothes on his bedroom floor. The sun was just coming up and his room was still quite dark.

He pulled his N.E.D. suit out of his closet and slipped it on, then found a large duffel bag on the floor behind his shoes. He unzipped the bag and emptied it onto one of the few empty spaces on the floor. Alex sat down and studied the contents of the duffel bag as if they were some archaeological discovery: his GameTronic portable video game device, a few dozen game discs, various adapter cords, wires, and headsets, and, finally, a stack of *VideoGamer Monthly* magazines.

As he looked down at it all, he got a tickle in his memory. *Did I really used to like video games?* He felt a sudden itch to flip through the magazines, throw in a disc, and play for a few hours. But he stopped himself. He had something far more important to do.

Alex rummaged through a pile of dirty clothes, found his damp, striped beach towel, and tossed it into the duffel bag. He opened his underwear drawer and grabbed the cleanest pair of tighty-whities he had. He reached under his pillow and pulled out the blue and silver Mexican wrestling mask his Uncle Davey had brought back from Guadalupe. He folded it gently and placed it along with his tighty-whities in a ziplock plastic bag. He threw it in the duffel bag,

zipped it up, and headed for the door.

The last thing he grabbed as he ran out of his bedroom was the summer camp brochure his mom had left for him to look at.

Alex's dad was downstairs in his pajamas, hot cup of coffee in one hand, game controller in the other. He'd just fired up the TV and was preparing for battle when he spotted Alex.

"Hey, big guy! You're up early. You wanna play?"

For a split second, Alex considered it.

"Maybe later."

Mr. Filby smiled, then noticed the duffel bag.

"Oh," Alex explained. "Mom signed me up for that supercool summer camp weekend sleepover in the park. I was so excited I couldn't sleep. I'm gonna head down there on my bike, pick out the best site, and see if I can make some new friends. Okay?"

"*Okay?* Your mom will be thrilled!"

"Yeah. I know. Tell her I'll see her on Sunday."

"Have fun, champ. Oh, and wish me luck. Today's the day I'm gonna defeat that stinky Leacacosian Emperor, I can feel it!"

As Alex started toward the door, something popped into his head. He stopped and turned back.

"Try using your Chromium Shield to deflect the Emperor's FusionBlasts back at the green crystal in the center of his third eye."

His dad gave him a surprised look. Alex smiled at him, then walked out the front door. *Where did that come from?* Alex wondered to himself.

Andretti's Pizzeria was the only building in Present Merwinsville that still stood in Future Merwinsville, preserved as an historical building.

Alex climbed up onto the rooftop of the old brick pizza place and found an air-conditioning vent. He stuffed the duffel bag deep inside and gave it a pat. "See you in a hundred years or so," he said.

Looking out across present-day Merwinsville, Alex could see nearly all of downtown. It looked so different without the shiny-white, football-shaped towers from the future. Alex wondered if a Klapthorian attack would destroy all those G'Dalien-designed buildings and if Future Merwinsville would then go back to looking just like this—his normal, boring little town. He shivered a little at the thought of this.

"Not on my watch," he said to himself.

He climbed down the fire escape ladder, got on his bike, and headed for his backyard jungle gym.

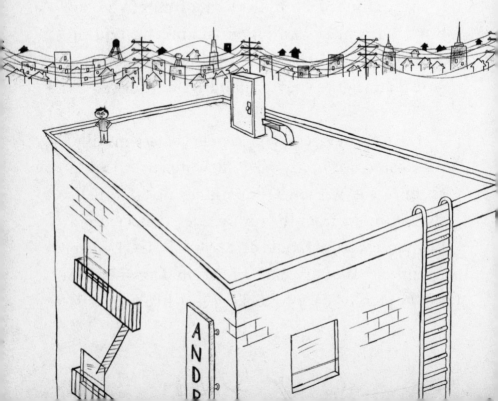

"Ew."

Sammi stood beside Herbert in the doorway, hesitating at the sight of Alex's incredibly messy bedroom. Taking a deep breath, they stepped over piles of clothes, toys, and leftover snacks, trying to avoid touching anything as they approached his closet.

"So if it's in here, we can conclude he's at camp, like his mom said," Herbert said. "If it isn't—"

"Just cross your fingers that it's in here," Sammi said.

"I don't believe in superstition. It isn't scientific."

"Neither is Alex. Do you believe in him?"

Herbert looked at her as he put his hand on the doorknob.

"I'm more curious to see if he still believes in us."

Herbert opened the door. Alex's N.E.D. suit was gone. Taped to the hanger was a note, scribbled in Alex's messy handwriting.

Alex popped out of the wormhole, rolled a few feet across the caveman diorama, jumped to his feet, and dusted himself off.

"Whoa! That was totally cosmic!"

A little boy about the age of Alex's little sister stood alone at the railing. His mouth was opened wide, and he'd just dropped his NeonPop TurboSucker.

"Wow! A real live AlienSlayer!"

Alex reached behind one of the fake rocks and pulled out one of the rubber G'Dalien suits Chicago had stashed there. He looked down at the kid staring wide-eyed at him.

"We'll see, kid."

He hopped the railing, picked up the boy's lollipop, and handed it to him. Then he ran down the Hallway of Human History, disappearing around the corner. The kid turned back to the caveman diorama and stared at the solid, black-painted, fake cave entrance, waiting for something else to pop out. A voice from far down the hall called to him.

"Sorry, son! That exhibit's temporarily closed!"

Dallas jumped out of the AirCart and began setting up the barricade. EL-ROY helped the little kid to the other side of the hall as Sausalito drew the curtain back.

Chicago hopped the railing and looked back at the kid before disappearing behind the curtain. "Gotta make a few repairs."

The kid turned to walk off down the hall. "No duh. It's *totally* leaking AlienSlayers."

Alex made his way through the squeaky-clean streets of Merwinsville, unnoticed in his baggy G'Dalien costume. He was trying not to look too panicked as he flopped his way toward Andretti's Pizzeria. By the time he ducked behind the historically preserved building, he was sweating swamp buckets.

Up on the rooftop of Andretti's, Alex shed his rubbery skin, stuck his hand inside the air-conditioning vent, and immediately pulled it back out. It was covered with cobwebs.

He took a deep breath. If he was going to be a solo AlienSlayer, he'd have to face much scarier things than cobwebs. He mustered his courage, reached back in, and yanked his duffel bag free from the sticky mess.

"*Yes!*" he said in a deep, action movie–type voice. "El Solo Libre triumphs once again!"

He shook off a century's worth of dust and grime and zipped open the duffel bag. His heart sank— he was met with a stench so musty and nasty it would've made his bedroom smell like a perfume shop.

Alex stared into his bag. It was covered with slimy greenish-brown mold. He mustered more courage, shut his eyes, and reached into the muck.

SHHLORRP! He pulled out the striped beach towel, which was completely covered in cold, green slime. He tossed it aside. *SPLAT!* It stuck to the wall of the stairwell. Alex slid his hand into the goo again.

He pulled the ziplock plastic bag out of the same moldy filth, wiped it off, and smiled as he unzipped it. Out tumbled his tighty-whities, as clean as the day his mother bought them for him.

"*Woo-hoo! El Solo Libre outwits the slimy green Mold*

Monster! Haven't even suited up yet and I'm two for two!"

He slipped the tighty-whities on over his N.E.D. suit, then looked down at the last thing in the plastic bag—the shiny blue and silver Mexican wrestling mask his Uncle Davey had brought him back from Guadalupe.

"Hola, *mi amigo*."

Alex pulled the mask on over his head.

His beach towel now a slimy heap of mold stuck to the wall, Alex was in need of a new cape. He came across a dusty old flour sack in a heap of pizzeria trash. The pull strings were torn and frayed but long enough for him to tie to the back of his N.E.D. suit. He fastened the cape, stepped back outside onto the roof, and walked over to the edge.

Feeling his mask on his face and hearing his flour sack cape fluttering in the breeze gave Alex a

unique sensation, to say nothing of the newness of wearing underwear on the outside of his pants. He stepped to the ledge and looked out at the city of Future Merwinsville.

He stared out at the massive, glimmering G'Dalien-designed buildings he'd imagined being wiped out by Klapthorian Death Cruisers. As he stood there, he vowed to protect them.

Past, present, or future, he thought to himself,

this is my town. My planet. My home.

"And no stink-suckin' space shrimp is gonna kick me and my friends off it," he suddenly blurted out. "Or my name isn't . . . *EL SOLO LIBRE!!!*"*

*Which, technically, it wasn't.

LO-PEZ was stuffed into the driver's seat of the mayor's newly waxed SkyLimo. Munching on a sandwich, he slammed the accelerator lever with his free tentacle and the towering buildings blurred past the windows. He licked a bit of mustard off his cheek and used another tentacle to jerk a red joystick to the right. The sleek, silent flying shuttle turned sharply, barely avoiding a floating MonitOrb advertising the Great G'Dalien Flee-Festival on Saturday.

Not that anyone sitting in the back could read

it. Herbert was pale and sweaty, groaning with each sharp turn LO-PEZ made.

"I can't believe you told Alex," Chicago said to Sammi.

"It didn't feel right to keep lying to a *real* friend."

"What's that supposed to mean?"

"Never mind. I didn't think you'd understand."

"Y'know what? Think whatever you want. *I don't care.* LO-PEZ, let me out of here, *now.*"

Without missing a beat, one of LO-PEZ's tentacles hit a switch on the console.

SPROING! Chicago's seat launched out of the SkyLimo, into the air, with Chicago in it. Sammi looked back and saw a tiny speck in the sky, then

a parachute pop out. Chicago drifted over the city.

"Neat trick. Thanks, LO-PEZ."

"My pleasure. I always thought you could do better."

"*Ugh, do me next. I want out of this thing . . .*" Herbert's eyes were shut tight and his cheek was pressed against the window.

LO-PEZ yanked back on the joystick. The mayor's SkyLimo lunged skyward so fast that Herbert felt like his stomach had dropped into his butt. He turned pale, put a hand over his mouth, and tried to think about ginger ale and salty crackers.

Sammi was sad about Chicago, but she was more worried about Alex. She stared out at the approaching SlayerLair atop City Hall, silently hoping he was there.

LO-PEZ parked the mayor's SkyLimo and immediately began turbo-vacuuming the sandwich crumbs out of its genuine Corellian-9 leather seats. His two young riders quickly thanked him for the lift and raced inside the SlayerLair.

Old Man Herbert looked busier than usual, and very concerned. Floating in front of SarcasmaTron, he worked the hundreds of switches and dials while keeping a close eye on the HoloScreen.

"Mr. Slewg!" Sammi burst in, looking around the room. "We're looking for Alex! Have you seen him?"

Old Man Herbert answered without taking his eyes off the HoloScreen. "No. Isn't he with you?"

Herbert slowly entered behind Sammi, holding his stomach. The color was just starting to come back to his face. "That needle-brain came through the wormhole by himself, in *direct violation* of the pre-agreed terms."

"I haven't seen him," the old man said. "And I'm afraid I have even more potentially troubling news."

He hit a button. SarcasmaTron beamed a holographic map of the Milky Way into the center of the room. Everyone gathered beneath the familiar planets circling overhead: Mercury, Mars, Earth, and Venus, all the way to the outer edges of the galaxy, where there loomed a dark, pointy-looking shape. It moved slowly but steadily toward the center of the room—and the planet Earth.

"What is that thing?" Sammi asked.

"It's either a very small, oddly shaped meteor,"

Old Man Herbert said, "or a very large, properly shaped alien attack vessel."

"But more likely it's a meteor, right?" Sammi asked.

"Oh, yes," said SarcasmaTron. "Because *so* many meteors nowadays are shaped like attack ships."

Herbert's face began to go pale again. "It's an *alien*?! A real one? But you calculated the chances of an attack at a *tetraquadzillion-to-one*!"

"And I can't tell you how embarrassed I am," the snide computer quipped. "Really. I can't."

Herbert began hyperventilating as he stared at the pointy black shape. It moved past Uranus and was fast approaching Neptune.

"Take it easy. Maybe they're friendly," Sammi offered. "Like the G'Daliens."

"Yes!" Herbert said desperately. "They're friendly, like the G'Daliens! If one alien visitor can be friendly, it's absolutely logical to extrapolate that a second visitor would also be—"

"*Greetings, inhabitants of Earth. We bring you good news!*" The voice interrupted Herbert's hypothesis. He smiled for a moment—until he saw the Klapthorian's creepy bug face.

"*This is your Klapthorian Confirmation for Earth's appointment to be annihilated tomorrow, between the hours of noon and four. We're happy to let you know that we are on schedule!*"

"Say, you were right," Sarcasmatron said. "They are friendly!"

Herbert let out a tiny squeal.

"Wait." Sammi stared up at the scaly faced captain. "What do you mean, '*appointment*'? No one here made any appointments with you!"

She looked around the room. Everyone shook their heads no.

"*IT WAS THE ONE WHO CALLS HIMSELF . . . 'EL SOLO LIBRE!'*"

The image on the screen fizzled again. Suddenly, they were watching a digital playback of Alex making his intergalactic crank phone call.

Everyone stood around the room with mouths hanging open, watching as Alex trash-talked an actual Klapthorian captain, double-dog-daring an entire species of alien warriors to attack.

"*SEE YOU IN ABOUT TWENTY-FOUR EARTH HOURS, DEPENDING ON TRAFFIC. HAVE A TERRIFIC DAY!*"

The image fizzled again and disappeared. Sammi was in a state of shock.

"We have to warn the mayor."

"Yes," Herbert said through gritted teeth. His face had its color back. In fact, it had gone from pale to pink, and was now headed toward a fire-engine ragey-red.

THEN WE HAVE TO FIND ALEX—SO I CAN KILL HIM BEFORE THOSE KLAPTHORIANS GET TO.

GRRRRRR!!!

$\mathbb{A}$ lex strutted down Main Street with his chest puffed out and his flour sack cape flapping behind him. Human and G'Dalien heads alike turned as he passed by. Many recognized the silver N.E.D. suit, and they cheered him on—at least until they noticed the Mexican wrestling mask and tighty-whitey underwear. Then their cheers would fade and they'd just stare.

"*Stand aside!*" he yelled heroically as he made his way through the confused crowd. "*EL SOLO LIBRE, COMIN' THROUGH TO SAVE THE WORLD!*"

The crowd parted. A mother G'Dalien gathered her four babies in her tentacles. Although he was *technically* solo, Alex knew he couldn't fight the Klapthorians *technically* alone. Problem was, there was only one person he now trusted. And he had a  strong feeling he knew where to find him.

Alex entered the Lunar Shuttle Station and stepped to the back of the ticket line. It was mostly made up of picnicking humans, G'Daliens, and their pets, off for a day of low-gravity family fun on the moon's LunaPark. Alex was the only one without a packed lunch, Golden Retriever, backpack, or Frisbee. He was also the only one wearing his underpants on the outside of his clothes.

The ticket agent was a slim G'Dalien with a bow tie and poufed-up toupee. His name tag read FRANK-LIN.

"*G'Day!* Headed up to the park, then?"

Alex locked eyes with FRANK-LIN. "Citizen! The fate of the entire planet lies in your hands! I'm looking for a sidekick to partner up with me and help save the world!"

FRANK-LIN blinked at Alex for a moment. "Oh. Well, thanks for asking, but I like my job here."

"What? No—I need you to get me to the moon as quickly as possible, so I can locate my partner!"

"Ah! That I can do!" FRANK-LIN began *clickety-clacking* at a million keys on the console in front of him. "All righty. I found you a seat at the front of the shuttle," he said sweetly. "Technically, you'll arrive one one-hundreth of a millisecond before everyone else. How's that sound?"

Alex looked behind him. The entire line of ticket buyers was staring at him. He nodded to the grinning G'Dalien.

"Great!" FRANK-LIN smiled. "One round trippy, then?"

"Yes, please." Alex thought for a second. "And an extra one-way ticket back."

Clickety-clickety-clack! FRANK-LIN's tentacles danced over the keys of his console. *Ding!* Two tiny tickets popped out and he handed them to Alex. "G'Day! *Next!*"

Alex boarded the shuttle and sat down in the front seat. His mask was itchy, his underpants were bunching up, and the other passengers were staring at him. *Tough it out, Libre,* he thought to himself. *You've chosen your destiny. These are the sacrifices that come with being a lone superhero.*

Hummmmm... The shuttle gently lifted from the launching platform. Alex looked out his window at the city below him. He wondered how much time he had before the Klapthorians attacked.

I sure hope this works, he thought.

The trip to the moon took exactly seven and a quarter minutes. It began with a great *WHOOSH!*, which kicked in as soon as the shuttle

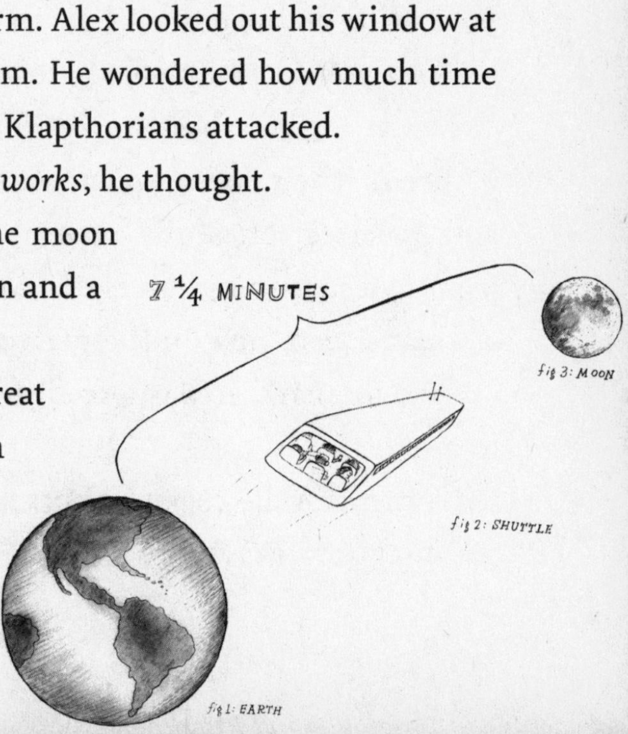

7 ¼ MINUTES

fig 3: MOON

fig 2: SHUTTLE

fig 1: EARTH

cleared the tops of Merwinsville's tallest buildings. As it broke through the Earth's atmosphere, the momentum of the soaring shuttle struck a soothing balance with the dropping gravity level inside the cabin. It caused an odd but pleasant sensation in Alex's belly, like the feeling he got in the backseat of his mom's car when she'd drive a little too fast over a rise in the road. He smiled as he thought of those little "belly tickle flips," as he and his mom used to call them.

Snap out of it! Your mommy's not here, Libre!

He shook off the memory and looked out the window just as the Lunar Shuttle was docking in the station on the moon.

Alex got up and pushed his way to the shuttle doors as they *whooshed* open. The park-goers gathered their pets, picnic baskets, blankets, and Frisbees, blissfully unaware of him. They'd experienced minutes on end of belly tickle flips as well, and were now in the perfect mood for a day at the LunaPark. It was a feeling Alex shared, but fought off.

Something he *couldn't* control were the effects of lunar low gravity, which hit him as soon as he stepped off the shuttle and into the moon's atmosphere. He took a deep breath and gulped a lungful of the cleanest air he'd ever tasted. Thanks to the oxygen-producing organic air pods the G'Daliens had injected into the moon's topsoil years ago, the air here was even purer than on Earth. Breathing it in only added to the calm, mellow experience of an afternoon at LunaPark. Alex exhaled and tried to ignore the urge to just lie down, relax, and stare up at the stars.

Bounding down the walkway leading away from the shuttle station, Alex's steps across the moon's surface were slower, but his leaps ten times as long. He had to fight the urge to do flips and spins in the air like a happy space dolphin as he focused on a sign at an intersection in the walkway.

The sign had two arrows. One said *LUNAPARK* and pointed off toward a charming, white picketed path made of glistening, polished moon rocks. It led to a large field lying within an enormous valley. In the distance, Alex could see visitors leaping around in the low-gravity atmosphere, building moon-dust castles, lying on picnic blankets, and soaking up moonbeams. Spotting a fun-looking Frisbee-golf game, he felt himself take a step toward it, then stopped.

SMACK! Alex slapped himself in the face. He turned his focus to the other arrow on the sign, which read, *DARK SIDE OF THE MOON*. It pointed down a craggy and rubbly path that, after about five feet, was completely engulfed in darkness.

Alex took one more deep, delicious breath, turned toward the wall of blackness, walked past the "KEEP OUT!" sign, and entered the dark side of the moon.

Herbert and Sammi climbed aboard the TransPodium to find Mayor CROM-WELL looking out over the busy Flee-a-seum. He was giving orders and artistic direction to the hundreds of BizzyBots zipping around the grounds, making finishing touches—hanging banners, filling confetti cannons, and polishing benches in the stands where the humans would watch the Great G'Dalien Flee-Festival.

"Just tell him!" Sammi whispered to Herbert. *"We have to get out of here and find Alex!"*

"Okay, okay, but we need to break it to him gently," Herbert said. "It doesn't help anyone if there's an all-out panic!"

"Who's doing all that murmuring back there?" Mayor CROM-WELL said, turning around. "Ah, our beloved AlienSlayers!" The mayor did a quick head count. "One, two—where's the mouthy one with the bad attitude?"

"I wish I knew." Herbert glanced nervously up at the sky, watching for signs of attack. He eyed a large bird suspiciously.

"Sir, we have something very important to tell you—"

"Of course! Gotta multitask, however! Lots to do, lots to do!" The mayor hit a controller on his TransPodium. Sammi and Herbert stumbled as the giant mobile stage lurched up into the air.

Sammi and Herbert steadied themselves like surfers riding a crazy wave as Mayor CROM-WELL recklessly steered the TransPodium above the field. They careened toward the oblong-shaped storage unit at the end of the Flee-a-seum and came to a jerking stop just inside, facing the InflataTron dutifully chugging away. Herbert nearly went flying into the half-inflated Klapthorian Winged Death Slug parade floatie, until Sammi grabbed his hand and yanked him back on board.

The inflatable Death Slug bobbed up and down on its rear end while its top half slumped over. Its batlike, leathery wings sagged sadly off its plump, mud-colored back.

"Your honor—" Sammi began.

"Isn't it gloriously hideous?" The mayor looked off and suddenly pondered, "Or is it hideously glorious?" He thought about it, then sighed proudly. "No matter! Either way, tomorrow this inflatable monster will mock chase the entire G'Dalien population into the Flee-a-seum, where the humans will mock welcome us with open arms. We'll then symbolically release the Death Slug into the sky and watch it harmlessly float away!"

At that moment, the inflatable slug's head flopped backward, revealing row after row of teeth circling all the way down its seemingly endless lumpy brown throat.

All three of them shuddered at the sight of it.

"*Brrrr*," Mayor CROM-WELL said. "Wouldn't want to meet one of those in the flesh again. I was a little boy, and I still remember the destruction it caused when the Klapthorians set it loose in our city. We fled just in time."

He turned to a pale-looking Sammi and Herbert. "But now that you AlienSlayers are here to protect us from any invaders, we'll never have to flee again!"

Sammi shot Herbert a look. He took a step toward the mayor. "Sir, I'm sorry to have to tell you this, but I'm afraid—*OW!*"

Herbert looked at Sammi. She'd stomped on his foot—hard—and now was holding a finger to her lips.

"*Shh.*"

Herbert watched in pain and befuddlement as Sammi gestured for him to follow her. Then she suddenly ran to the edge of the TransPodium and launched herself into the air. She landed safely on the storage unit floor, rolled to her feet, and ran out the giant steel doors, onto the field.

Herbert looked up at the mayor, who was artistically directing the BizzyBots to add more fake blood to the parade floatie's fangs. Herbert belly-crawled to the edge of the TransPodium and clumsily dropped to the ground.

"Ow!" He landed on his stomped foot and hobbled out the warehouse doors, trying to catch up with Sammi.

Mayor CROM-WELL turned around.

"Now then, what is it you have to tell me that's so important?" He stood staring at an empty TransPodium.

Back at the SlayerLair, Sammi was pacing back and forth. Herbert had his hurt foot soaking in a bright purple smoothie.

"We had a plan," he said. "What happened to our plan?"

"I know I said we should warn them. But you saw that thing! If that slug monster is what's coming tomorrow, there's nothing they can do!"

"Sure there is! They could do what they do best—

they could flee, *proudly*! Besides, there's nothing *we* can do, either! Or have you forgotten that *WE'RE NOT REALLY ALIENSLAYERS?!*"

"I know, I know. Let me think."

"Thinking is *my* department," Herbert said. "And I think we have to focus on finding Alex. If only because I can't wait to personally thank that nitwit for creating this whole mess."

Sammi looked at Herbert. Her face lit up.

"That's it," she said. "Herbert, you're a genius!"

"Well, *duh.*" He pulled his dripping, purple foot out of the smoothie and studied it.

Sammi spun around. "SarcasmaTron! Show me

the clip of Alex acting like a nitwit!"

"You'll have to be *waaay more specific*."

"The Klapthorian crank call from yesterday! *Quickly!*"

SarcasmaTron's HoloScreen beamed Alex's face into the center of the room, taunting the alien captain. Suddenly, GOR-DONNA leaned into the picture and spoke: *"I believe he said, 'space shrimp.'"*

"Right there!" Sammi yelled. "Freeze image!"

"Who's *she*?" Herbert asked.

"The one who helped, maybe even *tricked* Alex into starting all of this," she said. "SarcasmaTron, enhance."

"Oh yes, by all means let's get a closer look at the beauty queen."

He zoomed in. GOR-DONNA's ridiculously large, overly made-up face suddenly filled the room. Sammi squinted at it.

"Hey, I know that evil grin. SarcasmaTron, *baldify*."

The computer did as asked. GOR-DONNA's hair disappeared, revealing a bald, even more freakish-looking GOR-DONNA. Sammi peered closer.

"Okay. Now de-makeup. Replace with a nice,

healthy G'Dalien grayish-green, please."

The enhancement revealed a bald, makeup-less G'Dalien. It was GOR-DON, in all his olivey-evil glory.

"That GOR-DON creep?!" Herbert exclaimed. "He's behind this?"

"Shocker," SarcasmaTron said.

Sammi turned to Herbert. "GOR-DON is the key to stopping the attack *and* finding Alex. C'mon. He couldn't have gone far."

"Not in *those* shoes," SarcasmaTron said.

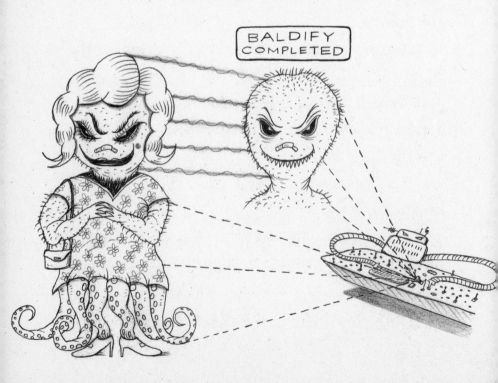

BALDIFY COMPLETED

Alex felt like he'd been walking through the blackness for hours. His eyes had adjusted as much as they could to the near-total lack of light on the dark side of the moon, but he could still only make out the vague shapes of the mountains, craters, and canyons as he trudged along.

It didn't matter that he couldn't see where he was going, because he didn't *know* where he was going anyway. But he could *feel* where he was going— and the feeling grew stronger with every step. Something out there in the darkness was guiding him in the right direction.

Hopefully.

Exhausted, he sat down on a moon rock and took a rest.

"Ow!"

Alex jumped up. Something had jabbed his fanny. He picked up a small, pointy stick. But it wasn't just any stick. Alex gave it a sniff. He smiled. He knew that smell anywhere.

"It's a SuperCheezyFrankOnnaStick stick!"

He jumped up and peered into the darkness, trying to see if there were more. There was barely enough light to see his hand in front of his face, never mind a small wooden skewer on the ground.

Sniff! Alex smelled the air. He sniffed again. Then he ran between two larger boulders, stopped, and crouched down. He picked up another SuperCheezyFrankOnnaStick stick, sniffed again, and began running full speed into a valley full of moon boulders.

WHUMP!

Alex slammed into something and bounced back, landing flat on his tighty-whities. He sat up and tried to focus on what he'd hit. It wasn't a moon boulder, or his head would hurt a lot more than it did. No, this was soft. And quite squishy.

And it spoke.

"You shouldn't be out here. You shouldn't be here at all." The raspy voice came from a shadowy, pear-shaped blob looming directly over him.

A terrifying *SQUEEEEAL* suddenly echoed through the cold air. Alex felt something big flutter overhead. "What was that?" he asked.

"Giant LunarMoths," the voice said. "Don't worry, they're not dangerous."

An even more terrifying noise echoed even louder. Something even bigger flapped past Alex's face, grabbed the LunarMoth out of midair, and flew off with it. *"What was that?"* Alex exclaimed.

"Giant MoonBat. They feed on the LunarMoths. Those are *very dangerous.* Come with me—if you want to live."

Wanting to live, Alex followed the pear-shaped figure, trying not to stumble on the rocky moon soil.

As they ran together, Alex heard squeals and shrieks all around him. He looked up. Every few seconds he could make out large, fluttering objects getting plucked out of the air by even larger flapping objects.

"*Okay. We're here.*"

They stopped. "Here" seemed to be a huge rock wall. Alex could make out a round boulder about the size of a beanbag chair sticking out of it. The figure pushed the round rock and it disappeared into a black beanbag-size hole in the wall.

"Climb in—quickly!" the figure said.

The two of them scrambled through the hole.

BOOM! Alex heard the round boulder slam back into the hole, plugging up the entrance.

If outside the rock wall was dark, this was something else. This was complete and utter blackness.

CRASH! "Ow!" He heard the voice on one side of him. "Who put that there?! Oh, yeah. Probably me."

SMASH! "Dangit!"

Alex stood perfectly still in the dark, listening to the stranger bang around his cave, wondering what would happen next.

Then there was light.

Tiny flames sputtered to life from small holes in the walls all over what Alex now saw was a cozy cave. Like hundreds of birthday candles, one flame seemed to ignite the next, until the entire rock room had a warm, orange, twinkly glow to it.

Alex turned around and took in the small, rock-carved room. He saw the beanbag boulder, tied with a rope and suspended from the ceiling, snugly plugging the circular entrance. He saw furniture, all carved out of moon rock, throughout the room.

Finally, he saw the mysterious pear-shaped man standing a few feet away from him.

Alex gasped.

The wrinkly old man had bushy hair on the sides of his head and a few scraggly strands combed over the bald part in the middle. His eyes were wide, and they looked familiar. Alex knew those eyes. He tried to think of where he'd seen them before.

Then it hit him—he'd seen them in his mirror.

This was Alex's 110-year-old self.

They stared at each other with mouths hanging open.

"*There's something weirdly familiar about this,*" both Alexes said at the exact same time.

NO WAY!

Old Man Alex's cave was almost exactly the same as Alex's bedroom back home. Except instead of furniture, most everything was carved out of moon rock. In the spot where Alex's bed should've been was a flat stone with a small boulder pillow.

Directly across from that, where Alex's desk would be, Old Man Alex had a squared-off rock desk and chair. And where Alex had his bedroom closet, Old Man Alex had carved a closet-size hole in the rock wall. It was cluttered with a bunch of junk, so you could hardly go in it, just like Alex's.

"This is so weird," Alex said.

"You're telling me!" Old Man Alex blurted. "I've never had a houseguest before."

"No, I mean you've made this place just like my bedroom."

The older Alex looked around his cluttered home. "Really? It kind of reminds me of my old bedroom—at least, I think it does. I can't really remember."

Alex's older self didn't seem very grown-up, especially for a guy who was 110 years old. By the looks of him and the way he spoke, Alex guessed he'd been alone in this cave for a long, long time. And by the size of his belly, Alex had a good guess who'd eaten all those SuperCheezyFranksOnnaStick.

"Hey—" Alex pulled the sticks out of his pocket. "I found these outside. They couldn't possibly be—"

"*SuperCheezyFranksOnnaStick!*" Old Man Alex exclaimed. He ran over to a small, shiny metal machine. It looked totally out of place amid all the rock-carved stuff in the cave. Engraved on the side of the slick, futuristic contraption was a logo:

SuperCheezyFrankOnnaStickerator 3000

"You want one? I can make tons!"

"No way!" Alex exclaimed.

"Oh. Okay. I thought maybe you were hungry, is all. You didn't have to yell at me."

"No, I didn't mean 'No way, I don't want one!' I meant, 'No way! A machine that makes SuperCheezyFranksOnnaStick!' Hook me up, old-guy-me! And don't skimp on the double-goopy SuperCheeze!"

Old Man Alex grinned as he excitedly slammed a button on the machine. The shiny box began to hum, and Alex smelled the deliciously familiar aroma of hot dog meat, goopy SuperCheeze, fresh-baked bread, and lightly toasted stick.

Ding! A fresh, hot SuperCheezyFrankOnnaStick popped out of the top, dripping with bright orange liquid cheese. Alex grabbed it and sunk his teeth in.

"Oh, *yeah* . . . " He grinned. "That's the stuff."

Old Man Alex beamed at his happy, younger self. His eyes lit up as he thought of something else.

"Ooh! Check this out—you're gonna love this!"

He excitedly bounced over to a rock wall. In a carved-out compartment was a sleek black console and a row of black goggle-like sunglasses.

A chunk of hot dog fell out of Alex's gaping mouth. "Whoa. My bedroom never had *that*."

Old Man Alex tossed him a pair of black goggles, which conked him on the head. The old man picked them up for his guest and put on a pair himself.

As soon as Alex slipped on his black goggles, the cave disappeared. Or rather, it *transformed*. Alex was completely engulfed in a perfectly realistic three-dimensional holographic battlefield. The sky was fiery red, with volcanoes in the distance. There were rivers of lava running through deep cracks in the black rock beneath his feet. Off in the distance was a jungle-like oasis. Beyond it, he could see a vast, dark ocean.

It all looked so real that Alex had to lift the glasses to make sure he was still actually standing in a messy little cave. He looked over at Old Man Alex, standing in the middle of the cave, wearing the goggles. Alex slipped his back on and slipped back into this incredible world.

"You ready?"

The voice belonged to Old Man Alex, but in this virtual world, he stood eight feet tall in full robotic body armor.

His battle suit was metallic blue and silver, fully loaded with built-in rocket launchers, blasters, and various other weaponry Alex couldn't wait to see in action.

"You look *awesome!*" Alex said.

"Thanks. So do you."

KA-CHUNGK! Old Man Alex's heavy silver boot took a thundering step forward. He spread his massive, silver chest plate so that Alex could see his reflection in it. His suit of armor looked like a mega-robot version of his El Solo Libre costume: his chest plate was his N.E.D. suit—silver with a tighty-whitey metallic band below his waist. He had a shimmering gold cape flowing down his back, which fluttered around his heavy plated boots.

Alex looked from his metallic exoskeleton to the incredible world around him. "What *is* all this?!"

"*This*—is the greatest video game in the history of video games! AlienSlayer43: Virtual Vengeance! You can modify your avatar however you want—I just had it scan and modify what you were already wearing. Hope that's okay."

"*Okay?! It's awesome! Let's do this!*"

Old Man Alex grinned, then touched a button on his silver neck plate. WZZZZT! Metallic blue and silver sections unfolded from his collar and assembled themselves around his head into a battle helmet. Alex smiled—it had the same blue and silver pattern as the Mexican wrestling mask his Uncle Davey brought him back from Guadalupe.

Old Man Alex's voice echoed inside his helmet. "Okay. Prepare yourself for Level One." He crouched into a ninja fighting position. A dozen or so weapons snapped and clicked all over his body—locked, loaded, and ready to fire at his command.

WZZZZZT! Alex did the same. His Mexican wrestling helmet clicked together, sealing itself around his head. He crouched into a ready position beside his older self. The two virtual warriors looked out at the vast horizon, where an army of dragonlike alien invaders came soaring over the volcanoes, speeding directly toward them in a menacing attack formation.

"Oh, *man* . . ." Alex giggled inside his helmet as he prepared for battle. "I'm so glad I found myself!"

CHAP
TER
30

Herbert and Sammi raced along Main Street armed with stacks of flyers showing a picture of GOR-DON. Printed beneath his grimacing face were the words, *HAVE YOU SEEN ME?* Since GOR-DON was someone most people in town did their best to avoid, the answer they kept getting was "no."

"Where is that nasty little blob?" Sammi said. "We're running out of time."

"Even SarcasmaTron couldn't get a lead on him," Herbert added. "He must be pretty well hidden. If he's even here."

Herbert and Sammi shared a worried look. Then they glanced up at the sky, nervously scanning it for signs of an impending attack. They quickly returned to handing out their useless flyers.

A crowd of AlienSlayer fans had begun following them through town. While none of them had seen GOR-DON, they had lots of wild theories on where they might find the crackpot G'Dalien.

"I got a whiff of him once," one man yelled out. "A mighty nasty stench, I can tell ya. My guess? He lives in the sewer!"

"No, no. He sleeps in the park—my dog peed on him once!" a G'Dalien mom yelled.

As they were steadily getting mobbed by more and more Merwinsvillians, Herbert grew more and more anxious.

"I hope Alex is okay, wherever he is," he muttered. He noticed Sammi giving him a surprised look and quickly added, "Only because he's wearing one of my N.E.D. suits. They don't just sell those things at the Merwinsville Mall, y'know."

"It's okay," Sammi said. "When we find Alex, I won't tell him you were worried. And we will find him."

Herbert gave her a smirk but said nothing.

A voice suddenly came blasting from the back of the crowd. *"Outta my way! President of the M.A.S.F.C.—comin' through!"*

Herbert and Sammi looked over to see a large woman plowing through the crowd. She wore a hairnet and an *I ♥ ALIENSLAYERS!* T-shirt, and had a large bag slung over her shoulder. She reached Herbert and Sammi, stuck out her beefy paw, and introduced herself.

"What an honor to meet you guys! *Marion Ploof,* newest president of the Merwinsville AlienSlayer Fan Club. Such an honor. Really."

"Uh, thanks," Sammi said, shaking her hand.

"Okay, so what do you need? Crowd control? I can have this place cleared in ten seconds. Transportation? Warm towlette? Water? Mr. Slewg, I've memorized your bio. I know you prefer sparkling."

As she began riffling through her bag, Sammi stopped her.

"That's okay, Marion. We're just looking for someone."

"A G'Dalien of interest," Herbert added officially.

Marion's eyes grew wide.

"You're on a *real AlienSlaying case?* Can I help? Oh, *pleasepleasepleasepleaseplease—let me help!*"

Sammi handed Marion a flyer and pointed to GOR-DON. "The only way you could possibly help is if you knew where this character is."

Marion looked at GOR-DON's picture and burst out chuckling.

"*Gordy?*" she said.

"You know him?" Herbert asked.

"Know him? We used to date!" She began riffling through her bag again. "He gave me his card. I've got it here somewhere."

Herbert stared at her. "Really? That's great!"

Sammi stared too. *"Really? You dated him?"*

Although Sammi and Herbert had walked through the Merwinsville Museum of Human History hundreds of times before, they'd never been there after hours. Closed for the night, its dimly lit, empty hallways were surprisingly spooky, even to them. When they stepped off the employee elevator into the dark and gloomy bowels of the building's basement, it was like stepping into another world. A very scary, slightly smelly other world.

They tiptoed around the huge Trash Disintegration Unit in the center of the room and found the door marked *KEEP OUT! TOXIC CONTAMINANT CLOSET!* Sammi checked the card Marion had given them. This was the place.

"Home Sweet Home," she said.

"You go in," Herbert said. "I'll keep watch out here."

"Uh, *no*," Sammi said. "You want to enjoy the benefits of being an AlienSlayer, you gotta earn them. We go in together."

She turned the knob. The door opened with a *creeaak*.

They stepped into the greenish-glowing, shadowy room and took in GOR-DON's tiny, nasty, messy lair.

"I didn't know Andretti's delivered," Herbert whispered, noticing the stacked pizza boxes.

"*Shh!*" Sammi peered into the dark room and stepped toward the green glow on the wall above the desk. They stopped and stared up at the holo-clipping display of AlienSlayer pictures, articles, and videos completely covering the wall.

"Wow," Sammi said. "Obsess much?"

Click!

Herbert squealed as the door locked behind them. They spun around to see a large, blobby shadow approach. It entered the green glow of the projections.

"Well, if it isn't the famous *AlienSlayers*," GOR-DON spat through a wide grin. "*I've been hoping you'd drop by.*"

The two titanium-armored SuperSlayers stood bravely on the beach of the small volcanic island and stared straight into the fiery-red eyes of the very last Three-Headed Aidanewellian Sea Beast. The gigantic, serpentine water alien burst out of the crashing waves and flew straight for them. Together they raised their shining silver arms. Missile launchers clicked up from their armor and locked in.

KA-BLATZ!!! ROOOAAAAAAAAARRRRGGGHH!!!
The ferocious Three-Headed Aidanewellian Sea

Beast let out a horrible wail as the Thermo-Blast Charges hit it in the chest and belly. It violently twisted and spun in the air, then crashed into the surf like a giant, scaly Viking ship. The monster plowed a fifty-foot trench in the volcanic beach, stopping dead just short of the two warriors' shiny silver boots.

One of the SuperSlayers turned to the other.

"Hungry?"

"Always. You thinkin' what I'm thinkin'?"

The two of them high-fived their heavy metal hands with a *CLANG!* and shouted in unison: *"SuperCheezyFrankOnnaStick break!"*

They pressed a button on their wrist control pads. The entire world they were standing in—the island, the dark sea, the dead Three-Headed Aidanewellian Sea Beast, *everything*—dissolved into a bright white void. Huge glowing words replaced the fiery sky in front of them: *"EXIT GAME? YES OR NO."*

The metal slayers fired quick WristBlasts at the word *YES.*

Alex and his older self took off their black goggles. Alex grinned as he flopped onto the moon rock bed.

"Wow! That was *totally awesome!"*

Ding! Old Man Alex handed his younger self a dog-on-a-stick. "Here ya go, partner. Extra double-goopy SuperCheeze, just the way you like it."

Alex chowed down the meaty treat in one bite and tossed the stick onto a pile of a few hundred in the corner.

"This is the best," he said, using his sleeve to wipe orange cheese from his mouth. "I totally get why you never leave here."

Ding! Old Man Alex smiled as he pulled out his own SuperCheezyFrankOnnaStick. "You mean why *we* never leave here."

Alex looked at him, then shrugged it off. "Hey, so is all that 'Fraidy-Cat Filby' stuff true? Is that why you went into hiding on the dark side of the moon?"

Old Man Alex scratched his head with a dogless stick. "That name kinda rings a bell, but I don't really remember. Hey, ready for another?"

Alex's mind began to race. Something wasn't right. He now remembered how much he loved video games, but it felt like that memory was blocking out another memory. A *really* important one.

"Hold up. So you don't remember coming here to get away from something?"

"Dude, I'm so old, I don't remember *coming here*."

The two Alexes stared blankly at each other for a moment. Then the older one burst into a big, goofy grin. "Who cares? Let's get back in the game!"

The game. "Hey," Alex said. "Where'd you get that AS43: Virtual Vengeance, anyway?"

"What difference does it make? I don't remember, okay? But if you wanna be Mr. Nosey, there's a note that came with it around here somewhere . . ."

He started rummaging through his stone desk drawer, throwing random objects around the room. Finally he pulled out a faded old piece of paper and handed it to Alex:

Dear Alex,

I know you're scared and lonely and feel like no one understands. But I do. When I get enough people to help us, you and I will lead the fight against the aliens. Until then, stay hidden and use this game to practice your alien—fighting skills. When it's time, I will send someone to bring you back.

Your old friend & neighbor,

"H. S."

Alex looked up at his 110-year-old self, who was holding out a pair of Virtua-Goggles to Alex, ready to go back in.

"C'mon! You heard the note. I'm supposed to be training till somebody comes. And it's *totally* working!"

Alex was in a confused daze. "What? What's working?"

"Our alien-slaying training! You saw us! We must've slayed half a dozen different aliens, each more powerful than the last! And it only took us seven hours! We kick butt! Up high!"

Alex stared at his older self holding his hand in the air. The weird feeling was growing stronger. Something was very wrong, but he couldn't figure out what it was. All he wanted to do was play AlienSlayer43: Virtual Vengeance again. He tried to shake that urge away. He had to concentrate.

"Hold on. So—what are you training for, exactly?"

"Man, your memory's getting as bad as mine, and you just got here! The note said I'm waiting for somebody to take me back to Earth and save everyone from the aliens, or something like that."

"Yes! That's it!"

Alex jumped up. His eyes popped wide open. His ears were ringing. He felt like he'd been hit over the head with a moon rock.

"Don't you see? *I'm the somebody!*"

"You're who, now?"

"The person sent to get you! *That's* why I came here! Merwinsville is about to be—*oh my gosh, what am I doing?! MERWINSVILLE IS ABOUT TO BE ATTACKED BY KLAPTHORIANS!* I came here to bring you back to help me! It's up to us to save everyone! *How could I have forgotten?!*"

Alex walked in circles, his mind racing faster and faster. It was all flooding back into his brain now, and he felt like he was waking up from a long and heavy sleep.

The older Alex munched on the SuperCheezy-FrankOnnaStick.

"Dude, you need to chillax."

Alex stopped pacing and looked around the room.

"*It's that game.*" He grabbed the note and approached the slick, black box on the rock shelf. He studied it like it was a dangerous weapon, then looked at the bottom of the note again. "'*Your old friend and neighbor, H.S.*' Herbert Slewg. But Old Man Herbert told me he didn't really know you. Why would he lie?"

"Herbert Slewg?—that name rings a bell."

"How did this game get here?"

"I don't remember. It just came, I guess."

"It just *came?!* It's not like the mailman delivers to the dark side of the moon!"

"It was a long time ago! I just remember playing. That's . . ."

Old Man Alex's voice trailed off. He looked up at Alex with a puzzled look on his face. "That's all I remember anymore."

They stared at each other. Suddenly, the two virtual alien SuperSlayers felt more like a couple of doofus-heads sitting in a tiny cave on the dark side of the moon.*

Alex took his Virtua-Goggles from Old Man Alex and dropped them on the cold stone floor. "Y'know what I think? I think you've trained enough. Look at you!" Alex continued. "Your whole life has slipped by while you were slave to a stupid video game!"

*Which, technically, they were.

CRUNCH! He smashed the goggles with his foot.

Old Man Alex looked at him. "What do I do?"

"That's easy," Alex said. "You just climb outta this hole in the wall, march into the light, and *go home.*"

"I am home. This is my home. It's where I eat, sleep, and slay aliens!"

"You don't slay aliens!" Alex said. "Not real ones! Trust me, I've battled *real* aliens and—" he stopped himself. "Well, up until recently I *thought* I'd battled real aliens, but it turns out it was just a video game."

"Kinda like me."

"Yeah. Kinda *exactly* like you."

"So you've never actually fought actual aliens, then?"

"No, I guess I haven't."

"And you're willing to do it now, to save the world?"

"Yeah, I guess I am. But only if you'll help me."

Old Man Alex slowly set down his goggles. He picked up a bowling ball–size moon rock. He took a deep breath and lifted the moon rock over his head, then hurled the mini-boulder across the room.

KRASHHH! The black AlienSlayers43: Virtual

Vengeance console exploded, spraying sparks and black glass all over the cave.

"One thing I learned getting to level ninety-three is you've gotta kill your enemy at the source. Or else they just keep coming."

"Okay." Alex grinned. "Good to know."

He pulled his blue and silver Mexican wrestling mask (the one his Uncle Davey brought him back from Guadalupe) out of his waistband. He slipped it on over his head. Old Man Alex's face lit up at the sight of it.

"Hey!" He rushed over and rummaged through his messy closet, throwing random objects around the room. He pulled out a torn and frayed blue and silver Mexican wrestling mask—the one his Uncle Davey had brought him back from Guadalupe.

"I always wondered why I kept this smelly old thing."

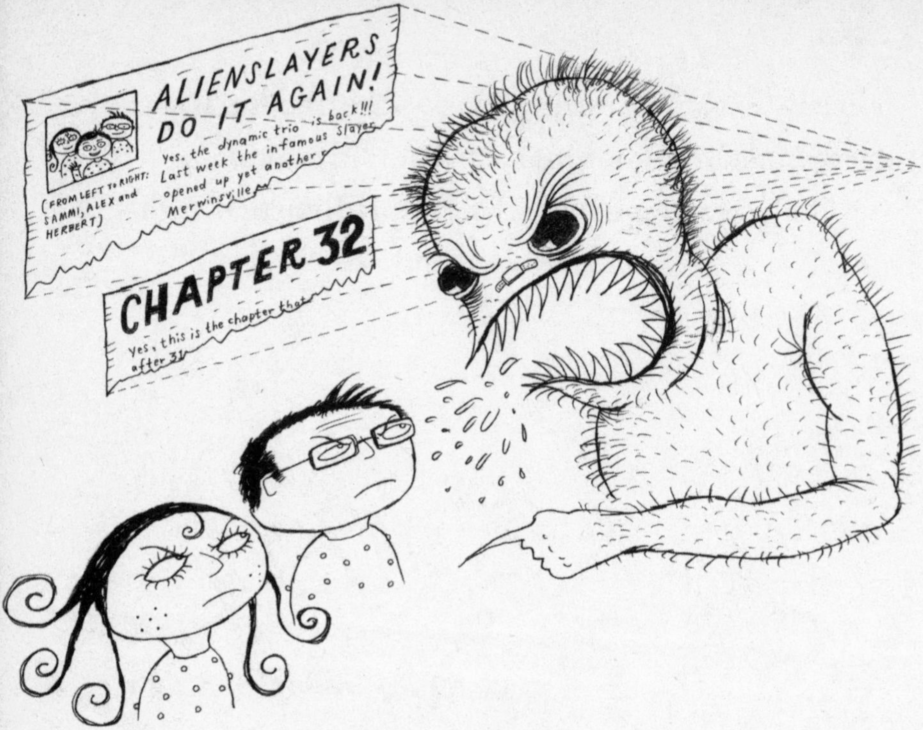

ALIENSLAYERS DO IT AGAIN!

Yes, the dynamic trio is back!!! Last week the infamous slayers opened up yet another Merwinsville...

(FROM LEFT TO RIGHT: SAMMI, ALEX and HERBERT)

CHAPTER 32

Yes, this is the chapter that after 31.

"Naturally, you're too late."

GOR-DON sneered as he stepped toward Alex and Sammi, into the greenish glow of the computerized news projections on the wall.

"Exactly what I'd expect when a *real* alien attack threatened a bunch of *phony superheroes*."

"WHERE'S ALEX?!" Sammi demanded.

"A-HA! You didn't correct me! That means I'm right! You *are* frauds, just like I've always said! YES! YES! YE— Wait. You don't know where he is either?"

"No. And FYI, we didn't say you were right," Herbert said.

"*You're a slayer short?!*" GOR-DON chuckled. "Oh, this has worked out even better than I planned!"

"If you know where he is, you'd better tell us," Sammi said. "And if he's hurt, you are *not* going to have a 'g'day.'"

"I haven't had a 'g'day' since you three *parasites* ruined my life! And as for your missing friend, I seem to recall him telling me he was going *solo.*" He turned to Herbert. "That was your suggestion, wasn't it? That's what your blabbermouth bodyguard told me, anyway."

"*Chicago,*" Sammi muttered.

"Has it occurred to either of you that maybe 'El Solo Libre' doesn't *want* you to find him? I mean, I'm a supergalactic mega-*jerk,* but even I wouldn't treat my friends the way you treated him. If—y'know, I had any."

Sammi and Herbert were quiet for a moment.

"All right," Sammi said finally. "Maybe it's too late to save our friendship with Alex. But it's not too late to save the world. So you're going to call off this attack—"

"Or else *what*? You gonna use your *megamittens* on me? *I KNOW ABOUT THE VIDEO GAME PRANK!* You two are about as good at fighting aliens as I am at baking cupcakes! It's over, losers, and I have won! Soon everyone who laughed and made fun of me will see that I was *always right*—the world-famous AlienSlayers are *superzeroes! BWAH-HAH-HAH-HAH-HAH!!*"

Sammi thought for a second. "And by 'everyone,' you mean everyone you're letting the Klapthorians wipe out?"

GOR-DON stopped laughing.

"Yes. About that," Herbert said. "You may want to rethink your evil plot. It has some intrinsic logic flaws."

"*Please.* Do you honestly believe I didn't plan *exactly* how to use the destruction of this pit of a planet to make myself Supreme Ruler of Gor-Donia?"

Herbert smirked. "*Gor-Donia?*"

"It's just a working title. I haven't made a final decision on the name yet. Although anything would be better than *Earth*. Why didn't you just name it 'Planet Dirt.' Oh, wait. Now I remember. Because humans are *idiots*."

Sammi stared up at the AlienSlayer news projections on the wall. Her eyes drifted down to a framed photograph standing on the desk beside the computer. She recognized the woman in the picture, and read the inscription.

To Gor-don, Love, Marion. We'll always have meatloaf mondays

"Okay," she said. "I'd just hate for you to go to all this trouble and end up with nothing."

"This room is designed to hold toxic waste!" GOR-DON snapped. "These walls are six feet thick! Whatever those psychotic shrimpazoids do aboveground, I'll barely feel a rumble down here. Once the Klapthorians have put their killer snail back on its leash, realized there's no LUNN-CHMUNNY to be found on this rock, then pack up and fly off to wherever they came from, I shall emerge from my bunker, rule all survivors of my species, and enslave all survivors of yours! Questions? Comments? *HA!* Didn't think so!"

Sammi picked up the photograph of Marion. *"Just one."*

GOR-DON froze. His beady eyes darted from Sammi to the picture and back again.

"Her? *Pff.* She knows how to reach me," he said, trying to play it cool.

"Yeah, we know." Herbert held up GOR-DON's business card. "She gave us your info. Funny, I don't remember her asking for it back, either."

GOR-DON looked at Sammi. His chin quivered.

"No, I don't think she did," Sammi answered. "Guess she's not interested in dating someone who's planning to destroy her planet."

GOR-DON suddenly snapped.

"*I told her I'd protect her!* All I asked is for her to come crawling back and help me reign over my kingdom of human slaves! So what's she do? She runs off—like *I'm the bad guy.*"

"Women," Herbert offered.

"I know, *right?* Can't live with 'em, can't eat 'em without getting a bunch of hair stuck in your teeth."

"Of course, there is one *sure thing* we girls can't resist," Sammi said. She let the words hang out there for a while. GOR-DON stared at her, waiting. Herbert seemed genuinely interested too.

"*. . . A hero.*"

"Yes! Which is precisely why my plan to *heroically* crawl out of my basement bunker and rule the Rubble Kingdom of Gor-Donia is *guaranteed* to make me irresistible! How could it not? She'd have to have a heart of stone."

Herbert and Sammi traded looks.

"Let me toss this idea out," Sammi said. "What if, instead of destroying Merwinsville, you were responsible for, I dunno, *saving* it?"

"You lost me. No idea where you're going with this."

She continued. "Let's say my colleague and I admit publicly, to everyone, *that we aren't AlienSlayers.*"

"Well, duh. I'd be instantly proven right, everyone would worship me, and Marion would think *I* was the hero instead of you—" GOR-DON gasped. "Okay. You just officially blew my mind. I order you to continue."

"Let's think this through," Herbert said. "Not only will you save face when we tell everyone we're phonies, you get to call off the Klapthorian attack and *actually* do what we fake AlienSlayers never *really* could!"

"You mean I'd—*save the world . . .*"

GOR-DON gazed up at the wall of holo-clippings and imagined all the headlines declaring him a hero. He could hear the adoring crowd echoing in his earholes. He could see Marion running into his tentacles. He shut his eyes. He could feel her soft, puddinglike lips kissing his.

AHEM.

Sammi and Herbert stood watching GOR-DON smooch his tentacle for an awkwardly long period of time.

"Ahem."

GOR-DON opened his eyes.

"We should probably head out if we're going to do this," Sammi suggested.

GOR-DON nodded. "Yeah. Okay. Right! Just let me slip on my dress and put on my makeup."

Young Alex helped his older self pull the beanbag-shaped boulder out of the hole in the wall. They swung it over to a wedge that held it in place. Alex stepped aside and gestured toward the cave exit.

"Age before beauty." He smiled. They were both wearing their blue and silver Mexican wrestling masks that their Uncle Davey had brought back for them from Guadalupe.

Old Man Alex took a step toward the hole, then pulled back. "I—I can't."

Young Alex looked at his older self's pear-shaped belly. "C'mon, you didn't eat *that* many SuperCheezyFranksOnnaStick," he said. "Suck in that gut. You'll fit through."

"No, I mean, I *can't*. I can't slay aliens, I can't go back to Earth, I can't step outside the dark side of the moon, I can't leave my cave. *I can't*."

"Of course you can! And besides that, you *have to*. I'm not gonna save the world all by myself!"

"I'm sorry," the old man said. "There was a time, years ago, when I probably should've put down the Virtua-Goggles, stopped eating SuperCheezy-FranksOnnaStick, and rejoined the world. But now it's too late. I'm just fat. And lazy. And I can't do it."

"Okay. I understand. I guess I'll just—*whoopsie!*" The younger Alex suddenly stumbled backward, tripped on a moon rock, and fell through the hole into the darkness outside.

"*Alex!*"

The older El Solo Libre rushed to the hole and leaned out. Two small, silver-sleeved arms reached up and grabbed him.

"*HUMMMPH!*"

Alex yanked his older self out through the hole with all his might. As the old man somersaulted in the moon dust, the younger Alex reached inside the cave and pulled the peg. The boulder corked the entrance hole with a *CRUNCH!*

"*What are you doing?!*"

Older Alex scrambled to his feet and rushed to the boulder. He pushed at it, but it wouldn't budge.

"Well," Alex said. "Looks like we're locked out. And—oh, no! I forgot my spare keystone." He burst out laughing. "Get it?! 'Keystone?!' C'mon. That's funny stuff. You need to chillax."

Old Man Alex wasn't laughing. Or chillaxing. He was freaking out.

"Why did you do that? Everything I own is in there!"

"Everything you own is made of rocks, dude," Alex said. "Except two things. You said you've gotten fat and lazy. Well, I think someone sent you the SuperCheezyFrankOnnaStick 3000 to keep you fat and the AlienSlayer:43 game to keep you lazy."

"Why would anyone want to do that?"

"To make sure you stayed in your cave and never came out. Because I may be a boring, normal kid, and you may be a fat, old, freaky, dim-witted hermit dude—"

"Hey—"

"—but I have a hunch that together we can do anything. Together, we can defeat any alien that dares poke their ugly snouts in our neck of the galaxy. Together, *we are EL SOLO LIBRE!*"

Old Man Alex smiled at Alex as he jumped up on a boulder and began cheering and waving his arms.

"LEE-BRAY! LEE-BRAY! LEE-BR—"

FLOOOMPH!

A black shadow swooped down and snatched Alex off the boulder and disappeared into the darkness.

"Alex? *ALEX!!!*"

Old Man Alex leaped into action, jumping from boulder to boulder as he chased the flicker of silver sailing away in the cold, dark sky.

"NOOO! ALEX! COME BACK!!"

"AHHHHHHH!!!"

Alex screamed at the top of his lungs as the giant MoonBat carried him over the craggy gray craters and valleys. Looking down, he spotted a tiny, pear-shaped figure taking giant steps in the low lunar gravity, trying to keep up.

"I'll save you, Alex! Just hold on!"

Old Man Alex suddenly skidded through the moon dust and stopped short at the edge of a very steep cliff. He looked up. He could only watch helplessly as the MoonBat carried his younger self away from him.

Soaring high above the canyon, Alex looked back at his older self stranded at the edge of the cliff, getting smaller and smaller in the darkness. He noticed the tiny figure lifting a large white object over his head. He was yelling something to Alex, but it was hard to understand. It sounded like . . .

"*Alex! Clock its gears!*"

"*What?!*"

"*Flock its beers!*"

"*WHAT?!*"

"*BLOCK ITS EARS!*"

This made only slightly more sense than flocking its beers, but Alex obeyed. He swung his body back and forth, gaining momentum until—

CLAMP! Like a real Mexican wrestler, Alex leg-locked the MoonBat's head. Then, like a kung fu master, he side-kicked his heels into the bat's huge ears. Alex squeezed his legs as tight as he could, plugging the creature's earholes.

SHRIIIEEEEEEK!!

The giant bat dove and spun, trying to shake Alex's feet out of its ears. It let go of Alex as it cut back toward the ridge where Old Man Alex stood. Alex hung upside-down, holding on by his heels. He spotted Old Man Alex spinning around with the large white object.

The next second, Alex noticed an *enormous moon boulder* soaring directly toward him. At the last moment, he popped his feet out of the MoonBat's ears. The animal's sensitive hearing picked up the ripples in the air as the boulder approached—but it was too late.

POOOOMPH!

The boulder slammed into the MoonBat and carried it over the far ridge of the canyon, leaving Alex to drop straight down toward the lunar surface.

"AAAAAAAAAAAA*aaaaaahhhh* . . . ?" Surprised that he hadn't hit the ground yet, Alex opened his eyes. Thanks to the low gravity of the moon, he was still falling—just veeerrrrrrrrry sloooowwwly.

As Alex gently floated toward the bottom of the valley, Old Man Alex calmly walked up and waited beneath him.

Alex drifted into his arms like a feather, and the Older El Solo Libre set him down on his feet.

Alex stepped out of the darkness and onto the shiny-stoned, pickety-fenced, flower-lined path that led off toward LunaPark.

He looked back. Old Man Alex stood in the darkness. He dipped his toe in the light. Then his foot. He lifted his leg in preparation and took a big breath.

"This is one small step for me, one gia—*whoopsies!*"

He lost his balance and fell into the light side of the moon. Alex looked down at him.

Herbert and Sammi weren't sure if Main Street was deserted because it was just before dawn and everyone was still in bed or because it was the 50th Anniversary of the Great G'Dalien Flee-Festival and everyone was already gathered in the Flee-a-seum.

Either way, as they clanged and banged through downtown Merwinsville in GOR-DON's junky jalopy, they were grateful to find the streets empty. Not only were they in a hurry to get back to the SlayerLair, but they would've hated for anyone to see them riding in a hunk of scrap with an evil

G'Dalien wearing a wig, a dress, and way too much makeup.

LO-PEZ was napping outside the ground-level entrance to the SlayerVator. He woke with a start and nodded to Herbert and Sammi as he crammed the last of an entire coffee cake into his mouth.

Then he spotted GOR-DONNA.

His eyebrows immediately started fluttering up and down on his puffy face like two caterpillars doing pushups.

"*Mornflub, M'amflor,*" he cooed to her through a mouthful of coffee cake. He swallowed the mushy pastry with some difficulty. "So nice to see you again, *m'lady.*"

"Out of my way, you moron," the gussied-up G'Dalien spat.

LO-PEZ watched as they zoomed up the SlayerVator. "Good looks with a dash of spice," he purred. "LO-PEZ *likey.*"

From his hiding spot behind a potted plant, Herbert stared at the Klapthorian's scabby brown face being holo-projected in the center of the SlayerLair.

"*Y'ello?*"

GOR-DON stood in front of the SarcasmaTron and addressed the alien receptionist in his best GOR-DONNA voice.

"Hello!" she said. "Could you connect me with the Klapthorian captain, please?"

"Ooh, I'm afraid he's out in the field today, with back-to-back annihilations. He's not to be reached, except in case of emergency."

GOR-DONNA looked over at Herbert and Sammi. They nodded "yes" frantically.

"It is," she said.

"Hold on. I'll try to connect you."

The HoloScreen image sputtered and went to static. Muzak played. GOR-DONNA gave a thumbs-up to Sammi, who was peeking out from behind the smoothie bar. He patted his yellow wig and turned to face the HoloScreen image.

The Klapthorian captain appeared, surrounded by knobs, lights, and various cockpit instruments.

"This had better be important."

"It is, oh huge one," GOR-DONNA said in an urgent-but-sweet tone. "It's about my son, *El Solo Libre.*"

"Oh! I know your son," the captain said pleasantly. "In fact, I'm on my way right now to destroy his planet and every living thing on it. How is he?"

"Not well, Your Immensity. That's why I'm calling."

"How can I help you, Mrs. Libre?"

"I know my son can be mouthy at times, but he's a good boy. He didn't mean to call you a shr— *whatever he called you.*"

"*I hate that name,*" the Klapthorian Warrior huffed.

"Yes, well, had he known that, I assure you he never would've said it. Especially to someone as *massive* and *gargantuanly mighty* as you."

The captain smiled a bit, but quickly shook it off. "I'm running behind, Mrs. Libre. What is it you want?"

"Only this, Your Largeness. Please, don't destroy Earth. I will see that the boy is severely punished, but please, spare our tiny planet. It would be . . . *so very big of you.*"

The Klapthorian captain was quiet for a moment. His beady yellow bug-eyes got a little more glassy than they already were.

"Y'know," he said, "I never knew my mother. She was eaten alive by me and my forty-seven thousand brothers and sisters, shortly after giving birth to us."

"Oh my, I'm so sorry."

"Don't be. She was . . . delicious." The bug-eyed commander wiped a small teardrop from his enormous glaring eyeball. "Mrs. Libre, your situation has touched me deeply. I have an offer for you."

"Thank you, thank you, oh giant one! Anything!"

"Let me take your mouthy, disrespectful son so that I can make an example of him by watching him slowly die in a horrible method of my choosing, and

I'll happily turn our ship around and spare your planet total annihilation. Deal?"

GOR-DONNA thought for a second. But only a second.

"Deal!"

"What?!" Sammi popped up and charged across the lair. "You can't let him do that! What about *our deal?!*"

"Excuse me, but who is this?" the captain asked.

"Just my daughter, sir. She has her brother's mouth."

"Such unworthy brats. You really do have your hands full, Mrs. Libre. A mother's job is thankless and never ending. Well, I'll be more than happy to help you by feeding your *other* burden to my pet Death Slug. Now where is the little scamp?"

"Ha!" Sammi said. "We don't know *where* he is, so there!"

"Hm. That does complicate things. I'm afraid if you can't produce El Solo Libre, we'll have to stay the course and destroy all of you."

"No. *Here I am.*"

They all looked over to the potted plant in the corner. Herbert stepped out from behind it and approached.

"Herbert, what are you doing?!" Sammi whispered.

Herbert looked terrified but determined. He turned to Sammi.

"None of this would've happened if I'd told Alex the truth like you wanted to. I was so concerned with losing the trappings of being a superhero, I didn't realize I was losing what it means to be a good person. It's my fault he's gone. I have to do this."

"You sound different," the alien captain noted. "Did you get a haircut?"

"What's it to you, *dendrobranchiatus?*" Herbert snapped, his voice cracking slightly.

The room fell silent. Herbert sighed. "Sarcasma-Tron?"

"*Dendrobranchiatus:* nerd-speak for the suborder classification containing such decapod crustaceans as the prawn, more commonly known as the *whiteleg shrimp.*"

The Klapthorian captain's bug eyes twitched. He slammed a switch on the console in front of him.

KA-ZZZZZZT!!

A blinding flash of yellow sparks suddenly engulfed Herbert. His body shook for a second as the light grew brighter and brighter. It sparked and fizzled, leaving a scorched circle on the shag carpet and the slight smell of burned raisin toast.

Herbert was gone.

"*Nooooo!!!*"

Sammi dropped to the ashy-black burned spot where Herbert had been standing seconds before.

"Well, that should do it," the captain said cheerily. "Mrs. Libre, you have yourself a wonderful day. You're a terrific mom, and your two children— oops, make that your *one child*—neither appreciates nor deserves you."

The HoloScreen went to static, and the Klapthorian captain disappeared.

The lair was filled with smoke. Sammi was crying on the floor.

GOR-DON was grinning.

CHAPTER 35

The Klapthorian Death Cruiser silently rounded the sun and pointed straight for Earth like a slow-motion arrowhead. It had no lasers, no missiles, no blaster cannons. It didn't need any of those things. Its real planet-destroying weapon, the Klapthorian Death Slug, was sleeping peacefully in its cage in the back of the vessel, like a family dog on a road trip.

At the front end of the Klapthorian Death Cruiser, in the very tip of its nose, was the teensy little cockpit. In it sat the teensy little captain and

231

his teensy little crew.

As universally feared as this ruthless species of space bullies were, the Klapthorians stood only about twenty inches tall. And they *really* didn't appreciate having that fact pointed out to them.

A Klapthorian first officer rushed to the thronelike captain's seat. The Klapthorian leader sat surrounded by lights and buttons in the center of the cockpit.

"Captain."

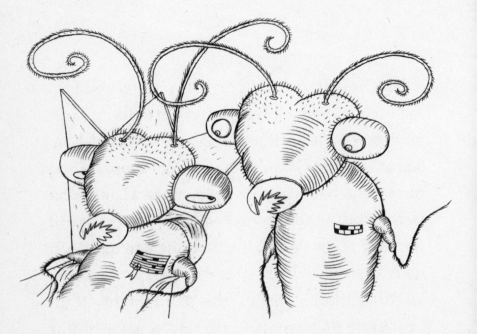

"Yes, what is it?" The captain sighed. He was a bit sad, because he'd recently been thinking about his mother.

"Sir, the human known as *El Solo Libre* has been successfully zapped aboard. He's being held in the brig, ready for execution."

"Let me ask you something, officer. When's the last time you called your mother?"

"Uh, sir, *our* mother's been gone a long time. We're brothers, remember?"

The captain looked closely at his first officer. "Oh, that's right. I thought you looked familiar. Sorry, Donald."

"It's Douglas, sir."

Herbert was stuck to a wall made of what looked like a beehive's honeycomb material. It was crusty and lumpy and had a funny smell. His hands and feet were held by the gooey gluelike slime that oozed from the porous walls. It wasn't comfortable.

A voice suddenly echoed from somewhere, startling him.

"What an honor. El Solo Libre, the greatest AlienSlayer in all the universe, right here on our humble Death Cruiser."

The captain's voice sounded close, but Herbert couldn't place where it was coming from.

Then he looked down.

The buglike leader stood at about Herbert's knees, grinning, with a few officers. They looked like a tiny group of angry insect elves.

"Oh, there you are. Didn't see you way down there."

The Klapthorian captain's grin disappeared. His tiny face grew dark. The officers slowly backed away from him. Four fluttering insect wings sprung from his back.

BZZZZZZZ . . . In an instant, the Captain was hovering in the air, right up in Herbert's face.

"Sorry, I didn't mean that as an insult, I just—"

"*SILENCE!* Your mouth has gotten you into enough trouble, *AlienSlayer*. It nearly cost you your planet, and now it will cost you your life. To say nothing of the pain you've put your mother through."

He buzzed to the other Klapthorian officers. They swarmed around a lever and pulled it down. The floor beneath Herbert disappeared. He hung suspended in the goopy wall above an enormous but oddly familiar-looking creature, sleeping soundly in his cage below. Herbert caught his breath.

"Is that a real Klapthorian Death Slug?!"

"You do know your aliens, *slayer*." The captain chuckled, still fluttering in Herbert's face. "So you must also know that there's nothing *Mr. Nibbles* enjoys more after a long nap than a nice, juicy, Klapthorian nectar-dipped hunk of *raw meat*."

A million things raced through Herbert's mind, but one odd thought in particular really annoyed him: *He was about to become a human-size, honey-dipped, SuperCheezy-HERBERT-OnnaStick.*

"Well, this is ironic," he muttered to himself.

SHLLLLLUUUP! The ooze holding Herbert's hands and feet made a horrible sucking noise as it began to withdraw back inside the walls.

Herbert tried to hold on to the slime, but it was like trying to grab a fistful of snot. The goo slipped through his fingers, and he fell through the trapdoor. As he did, he reached out and grabbed something.

BZZZZZTTT!!!

Herbert was gripping the tiny, kicking legs of the Klapthorian captain.

As the two of them dropped straight for the sleeping Death Slug's head, the captain violently flapped his tiny wings like he'd never flapped before. His efforts slowed their fall to a stop in midair, where they hovered unsteadily just above the horrible creature's head.

BZZZZZZZ-ZZZZZZT!

The giant worm stirred at the buzzing near its earhole, and rolled over on its back.

SKRONK! Its snore rattled the cage, leaving its mouth wide open. Herbert tried not to squeal as his feet dangled just above the gaping mouth full of spiraling razor teeth.

The Klapthorian captain began yanking at Herbert's hair.

"Ow!"

Herbert let go with one hand and swung on the captain's feet with the other, throwing the struggling little bug alien into a tailspin. The two of them slammed into the side of the cage, and Herbert dropped to the floor. Finally free, the Klapthorian captain shot straight up through the trap door, shaken but glad to have gotten away.

Mr. Nibbles opened his horrible mouth so wide the mayor's SkyLimo could've parallel-parked inside. Herbert clenched his eyes shut and prepared to be eaten.

YAAAAAAWWWWWWNNN! The Klapthorian Winged Death Slug rolled over again and fell back asleep.

The officers buzzed around their dear leader, checking him for any injuries as they rushed him off toward his tiny cockpit.

"Who knew El Solo Libre was so cunning! It's fortunate we destroyed him before he could attack us."

"Planet Earth dead ahead, sir. Awaiting your orders."

The captain sat up slowly. He focused his gaze out the cockpit window, past the moon, at the Earth in the distance.

"LUNN-CHMUNNY reading?"

"I can't find any LUNN-CHMUNNY, sir."

"I won't break a promise to a mother. Pull a U-turn around that small, white rock up ahead. Let's head home."

The two Alexes sat on a smooth, flat moon rock just outside the LunaPark Shuttle Station, staring into space.

Old Man Alex pulled off his shoe and poured out a pile of moon dust. "Nothing to be done."

"I can't believe this," Alex said. "What time do you think the shuttle starts running?"

"For the hundredth time, I don't know."

"Well, you live here."

"Not *here*. In a cave. On the dark side of the moon. For about fifty years. Doesn't exactly make me the *shuttle schedule guy.*"

They stared out at Earth. The sun was shining its light on one side of the blue planet. It looked beautiful.

"It's morning in Merwinsville," Alex said.

"Yep."

A shadow began to creep across them, turning the light side of the moon suddenly dark. The older Alex looked around.

"Man, *that* day flew by, huh?"

"Wait a minute . . ."

Alex stood and turned around. The darkness was blanketing everything—nearby craters, moon mountains, even LunaPark. He looked up.

The Klapthorian Death Cruiser floated ominously overhead.

"*Oh no . . . that's them! We're too late!*"

Old Man Alex jumped to his feet.

"We have to do something!"

They both stood gaping at the massive ship making its way past them overhead. Alex's mind was racing. He glanced around frantically. Nothing but rocks, rocks, and more rocks.

"*The boulders.* Like you did with the MoonBat!"

"Okay, but I really don't see how tagging another MoonBat with a boulder is gonna do anything."

"No! Throw one at the ship! *A big one!*"

"Oh, right. See, now that makes a lot more sense."

Alex began running. "C'mon! If you can hit a MoonBat fluttering around in the dark side of the moon, you can easily hit *that* thing!"

The enormous ship was still passing overhead. It was almost bigger than the moon itself. Old Man Alex narrowed his gaze as he stared up at it.

"Okay. *Boulder me!*"

The two of them leaped up and over the side of a large crater. Inside were hundreds of boulders lying around in all sizes and shapes. Alex ran over to a big one.

"Here! Quick! Throw this one! Now!"

"*Meh,*" Old Man Alex said. "That one's kinda lumpy."

NAH.   TOO ROUND.   TOO LUMPY.   TOO BLAH.   TOO SMALL.

"Fine!" Alex yelled. "You pick one, then! Just hurry!"

The back of the ship now finally came into view across the lunar valley. Old Man Alex walked over to an enormous boulder. He hoisted it up over his head and began to spin around inside the crater, faster and faster. A dust swirl whipped around him. It soon looked like a boulder floating atop a small cyclone.

HUUUURRRRMMMMPPPHHHH!

Old Man Alex let go of the house-sized moon rock, hurling it straight at the Klapthorian Death Cruiser. As the dust settled around them, they stared up at the projectile. It faded, growing smaller and smaller as it floated toward the massive ship gliding silently overhead. By the time it reached its target, the moon boulder looked about the size of a golf ball. The ship was farther away—and much, much bigger—than either of the Alexes realized.

"Ohpleaseohpleaseohpleaseohpleaseohpleaseoh-please—"

Ping.

It tapped the rear end of the Klapthorian Death Cruiser's hull like a mosquito bumping into a bus.

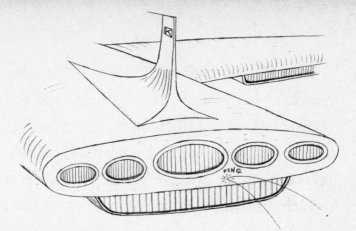

But it was enough.

Bright red brake lights lit up the back of the ship, casting a ruby-red glow across the entire face of the moon. The ship stopped in midair above them—and began backing up.

BEEP! BEEP! BEEP! BEEP!

"Uh-oh," Old Man Alex said.

"Uh-oh," Herbert said.

In the belly of the cruiser, he'd been slowly, carefully, quietly tiptoeing around the snoozing Klapthorian Winged Death Slug, careful not to wake it as he searched for a way to escape.

When the ship suddenly jerked to a stop, it slammed the nasty worm's head into the wall and woke it with a jolt.

"RRRRROOOOAAAAAARRRR!!"

Mr. Nibbles stirred, rising up on his tail, thrashing his head around in the air, and gnashing his pitlike mouth full of teeth.

Herbert froze. The slug spread its leathery wings behind it and sniffed the air. It shifted its massive body around and focused on Herbert crouching in the corner.

"Nice sluggy-wuggy . . . ? H-h-how was your n-nap, big fellah?"

"RRRRREEEEEEEEOOOOOOOOOAAAAARRRR!!"

In the Klapthorian cockpit, the captain's tiny bug eyes were peering at a small screen. Two small, silver-clad figures were jumping up and down on the surface of the moon.

"Enhance image," he said. "And give me sound."

His first officer worked some dials and buttons. The image zoomed in. The two silver-clad figures' voices could be heard through the Klapthorian cockpit speakers. Alex was doing most of the yelling.

"Yeah! How'd you like that, huh?! You want some more?!"

"Wait. I know that taunting voice," the captain said.

"You're messing with *Los Solo Libres* now!" Alex continued, leaping up and down inside the crater as Old Man Alex joined in.

"That's right! Think you're big and tough?! Come on down here and have a piece of this, *space shrimps!*"

Everyone in the cockpit froze.

The Klapthorian captain trembled with rage. He turned to his officers.

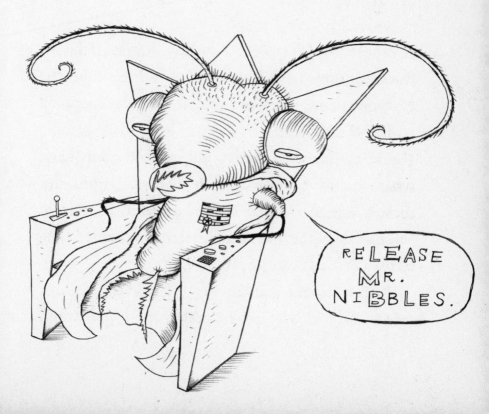

RELEASE MR. NIBBLES.

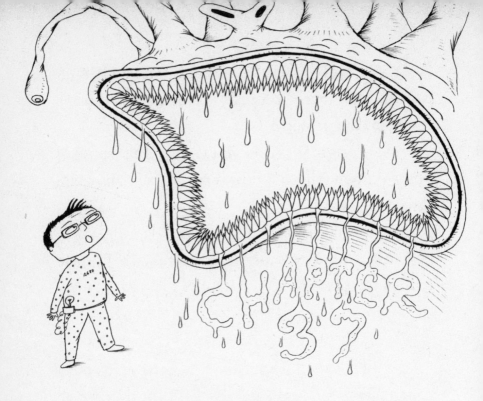

CHAPTER 37

Herbert was terrified. Fighting for his life, he dodged, dove, ran, and rolled all around the cavernous cage, barely avoiding the hungry snapping jaws of Mr. Nibbles.

He managed to scurry behind the giant slug, where he was able to catch his breath, if only for a half second. As the beast lumbered around to relocate his after-nap snack, Herbert grabbed hold of the tip of his lumpy tail.

This was not a good move.

Mr. Nibbles felt Herbert grab him. In an instant,

he snapped his tail upward, flinging Herbert high into the air.

"AAAAHHHHHH!"

The giant blob spun around and positioned his horrible mouth beneath Herbert, who saw the concentric rows of teeth circling deep into the depths of the huge slug's throat. *This is it*, Herbert thought as he began to fall. He shut his eyes tightly and waited for the sound of his own crunching bones.

WOOOOOOSSSHHH!

A strange chill suddenly filled the air, and a sucking sensation seemed to pull him downward even faster. Surprised he wasn't being chewed yet, he opened his eyes.

Herbert was still falling toward Mr. Nibbles, but the confused creature was now also falling, beneath and away from him at a rapid pace. The bottom of the cage had disappeared. Both Herbert and Mr. Nibbles were steadily floating down onto what looked like the surface of the moon.

The giant Death Slug spun its body around and spread its leathery wings. As it stopped its slow, low-gravity fall, Herbert landed square on its back with a gentle bump—and grabbed hold of its mealy back flesh.

Mr. Nibbles touched down near the LunaPark Shuttle Station, where the day's first shuttle, full of early-bird picnickers and park-goers, was just coming in for a landing. The grouchy slug-beast turned to it and let out a horrible, shrieking "RRROOOOOOOOOAAAARRRR!!"

Everyone on the shuttle screamed back in horror as the angry space worm charged the vessel. He raised himself on his tail, using his wings to balance as Herbert clung to his back.

Mr. Nibbles took one last giant spring and went to lunge mouth-first at the shuttle full of innocent picnickers.

BONK!

A large boulder bounced off the side of the space worm's head, knocking him off course. He missed the shuttle completely. Herbert was tossed off and went sliding onto the dusty surface of the moon. He stood up as Mr. Nibbles spun around, and they both stared in disbelief at the same sight.

Two weirdos wearing Mexican wrestling masks on their heads stood atop the edge of the crater, striking a dynamic, super-duo pose.

"What in Newton's name?" Herbert muttered.

"*RRRRREEEEEEEOOOOOOOOOOAAAARRRR!?!*" Mr. Nibbles added.

The Klapthorian Death Slug charged the two Alexes, spreading its wings as it leaped in the air.

"Boulder?!" Old Man Alex asked.

"Not this time," Alex replied. "*RUN!!*"

The two of them slid down the crater just as Mr. Nibbles *CRASHED* headfirst into its side. They ran beneath him and bounded back to the Lunar Shuttle full of still-screaming passengers, and grabbed Herbert as they passed him.

"Wait! Don't go!" Alex cried out to the shuttle.

"Alex?! Is that you?"

"Hold the train!" hollered Old Man Alex.

Herbert looked at the masked weirdo holding his other arm. "All right. I officially have no idea what is going on."

Mr. Nibbles was slightly dazed from his crater-cranium crunch and turned slowly to focus on his three snacks as they jumped onto the shuttle full of picnic-bound passengers. He shook off his dizziness, bounced into the air, and spread his wings. In a second he was lunging toward the slow-moving shuttle as it lifted off toward Earth.

On board the cruiser, the Klapthorian captain couldn't believe his bulgy bug eyes as he watched his pet slug chase a tourist shuttle toward Earth. Even worse, it was a shuttle he knew was transporting the *real* El Solo Libre.

"We were *tricked*," he seethed. "Full speed ahead—*follow that Death Slug!*"

Sammi was still in shock, thinking about Herbert even as GOR-DON dragged her up onto the TransPodium. It was parked in midair above the floor of the Flee-a-seum, facing the human crowd waiting in the stands for the big celebration to begin.

Mayor CROM-WELL waved and grinned his pearly square teeth at the crowd, soaking in their cheers as he prepared to kick off the festivities. Just outside, the G'Dalien population was waiting for his signal to begin their Great Flee enactment parade into the Flee-a-seum.

"Quick! Before that windbag starts blabbing!" GOR-DON shoved Sammi toward the mayor. "We had a deal—now *tell them!*"

Sammi was too upset to fight the evil G'Dalien. Alex was missing. Herbert was gone. She wanted more than anything to undo everything that had happened. Deep down, she wished with all her heart to just tell everyone the truth and get everything to go back to normal again. If it meant never going through the wormhole ever again, that would be fine with her.

"Excuse me, Mr. Mayor. May I please make an announcement?"

Mayor CROM-WELL frowned a bit and consulted a long schedule he carried with him. "It's not on the Flee-Festival Program—"

"Please, sir. It's important. I'll be quick."

Mayor CROM-WELL stepped aside and gave Sammi the stage. The crowd broke into a loud cheer as they recognized the AlienSlayer. Their reaction made her feel worse about what she was about to tell them. Her small voice echoed across the jam-packed arena.

"Um, I need to say something that should've been said a long time ago. This isn't easy, but here goes. I'm sorry that my partners—my best *friends*—couldn't be here today . . ."

Sammi felt a lump in her throat as she tried to hold back her tears. She couldn't believe this was happening.

"Stupid sentimental humans!"

GOR-DON bumped her aside as he addressed the crowd. "What she's pathetically *failing* to say is that I, GOR-DON, was right all along—the AlienSlayers are *FAKES!*"

There was a half second of silence. Then the crowd burst out laughing. GOR-DON was confused. He glanced down at himself.

He was still dressed as GOR-DONNA.

"Silence!" he yelled as he yanked off his wig. "Stop laughing! *LISTEN TO ME!*"

The crowd continued to laugh, boo, and taunt him—until a voice stopped them cold.

"He's right."

Sammi stepped beside the seething alien and looked out at the stunned crowd. "We're not AlienSlayers. We never were. We're just three normal, boring kids. We tricked you all and we're—*I'm*—so sorry."

Sammi hid her face in her hands and turned away. Rushing toward the back of the TransPodium, she bumped into Chicago. He put his arms around her and let her cry into his shoulder.

"That was good," he said. "You did the right thing."

"What are you doing here?"

"I heard about Alex and Herbert. I'm so sorry— about everything. C'mon. I'm getting you outta here."

GOR-DON stood in front of the stunned crowd, his prickly bald head throbbing. Mayor CROM-WELL looked at the schedule for the fifth time in five minutes, then back to the G'Dalien in lipstick and lady clothes standing next to him.

"I don't understand. None of this is on the program."

GOR-DON slapped the schedule out of his hands. "This is my show now," he hissed. He turned to the crowd of confused humans in the stands.

"*HUMANS!* You now know the truth! The AlienSlayers tricked you all! *I am your hero!* It is I

256

who stopped an actual alien attack, scheduled between noon and four this very afternoon!"

As he spoke, the G'Daliens began pouring onto the floor of the Flee-a-seum. They were tired of waiting outside for their signal and wanted to know what all the shouting was about.

GOR-DON saw them and continued, pointing up at the blue sky.

"If not for my bravery and superior wisdom, all of you, humans and G'Daliens alike, would have been helpless against a deadly and destructive attack from above!"

Everyone looked up at the sky. At the same spot in the sky. Some pointed to the spot in the sky. The spot in the sky was getting larger. And closer.

"And now, thanks to me, *your new leader*, you're safe from—"

The Lunar Shuttle suddenly slammed into the ground of the Flee-a-seum, sending the G'Daliens scrambling for cover. It skidded to a stop along the dirt floor, its nose half buried in the dirt and its rear end tilting up in the air. The screams of the crowd quieted into confused mumblings.

KUNGK! The back panel of the shuttle popped off.

The crowd fell silent—until Herbert and Alex popped their heads out. A burst of cheers filled the Flee-a-seum.

Mayor CROM-WELL picked up his Flee-Festival schedule and studied it again. GOR-DON stared out at the field in disbelief.

"Alien Slayers?!"

Sammi couldn't believe her eyes. She laughed through her tears at the sight of Alex and Herbert— until she noticed they were ignoring the cheering crowd. They were frantically pulling passengers out of the back end of the shuttle. Something was wrong.

Sammi peered up and spotted it—a huge, winged, brownish blob diving toward them, coming in fast.

"Oh, no." In an instant, she backflipped off the TransPodium and raced toward her friends in the center of the Flee-a-seum.

"Hurry!"

Inside the shuttle, Old Man Alex helped the last picnicker climb toward Herbert and Alex, who pulled him out to safety.

Alex and Herbert reached in and struggled to

pull Old Man Alex's heavy, pear-shaped body up and out of the back of the shuttle. Sammi jumped aboard and tugged with them. Looking over her shoulder, she saw the huge blob coming straight for them. It was so close she could see its sinkhole of a mouth, full of teeth, wide open and ready to devour them like a tube of Slayer-Snacks.

"Time's up!"

She stopped tugging and suddenly *shoved*.

Sammi, Alex, and Herbert all fell *into* the shuttle. They slammed into Old Man Alex, and the four of them tumbled toward the grounded front of the small ship.

"Quick! Out the windows!"

"RRRRREEEEEEEOOOOOOOOOOAAAARRRR!!" The gigantic winged worm bashed into the back of the shuttle like a roll of cookie dough being crammed into a toothpaste box.

The four of them swung themselves out the windows and onto the roof, just as Mr. Nibbles' crashing momentum thrust the shuttle across the Flee-a-seum field. Herbert, Sammi, Alex, and Old Man Alex held on tightly as the slug-stuffed shuttle plowed past the stunned crowd. It careened toward the oblong-shaped building at the opposite end of the field. They ducked just in time as it blasted through the warehouse doors and disappeared inside.

KA-CHUNGK!

Mr. Nibbles' head slammed into the heavy InflataTron. Attached to it was the fully inflated Death Slug parade floatie, bouncing gently and light as air.

Mr. Nibbles, the real Klapthorian Winged Death Slug, lay beneath it, wrapped tightly in the twisted metal Lunar Shuttle cocoon, knocked out cold. Herbert looked from the unconscious beast to his life-size floatie twin.

"Again, ironic."

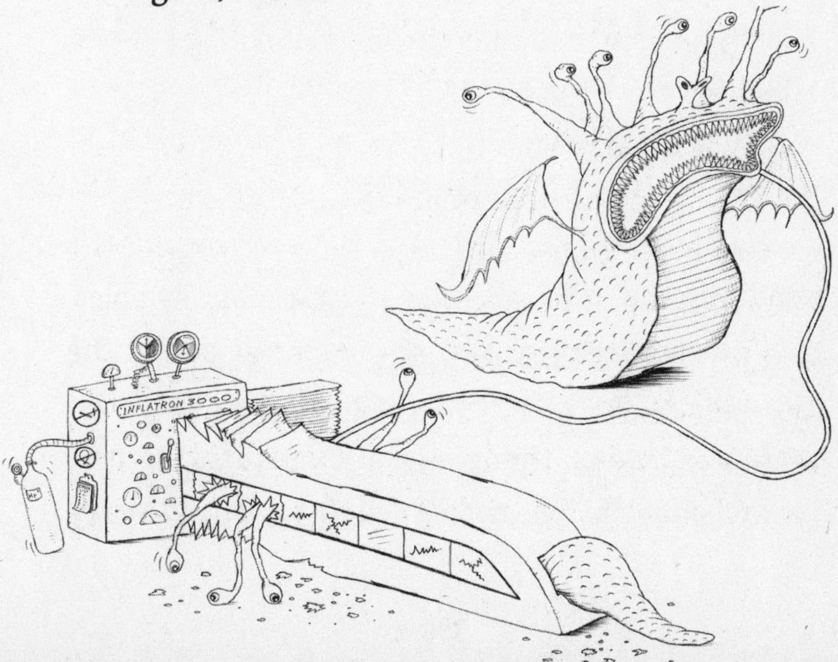

Alex climbed off the motionless monster, stepped back, and joined Herbert, who was staring at Mr. Nibbles.

"Whoa," Alex said.

"Try being his roommate," said Herbert.

Sammi climbed off and said nothing. She stepped up and hugged her friends—very tightly, and for quite a long time. She only stopped when she felt a fourth pair of arms join the embrace.

She pulled back and looked at the large, doughy man in the moon dust–soiled Mexican wrestling mask.

"Um . . . sorry. Who are you?"

Old Man Alex pulled off his mask and gave them a big, goofy grin. A grin they recognized even beneath a century of wrinkles.

"No way."

Old Man Alex studied Sammi's face. "You look *really* familiar," he said. "Have we met?"

Sammi looked up at Alex. "You did it! You found yourself!"

Alex shrugged and began walking away.

"Hey, where are you going?" Herbert asked.

Alex slipped his mask on. "I'm going solo," he said, and headed for the smashed hole in the door.

FWAP! A much older, grimier, stinkier mask tagged him in the back of the head. He spun around. Old Man Alex shrugged and pointed at Sammi. She looked madder than he'd ever seen her.

"You're being such a—a *doofus*!" She hollered at him. "Who do you think you are?"

"*El Solo Libre.* The greatest AlienSlayer in the galaxy."

"Give me a break! You're Alex Filby! You live next door to me on Sherwood Circle, you only took the training wheels off your bike last summer, *and* you still sometimes wake up crying for your mommy in the middle of the night whenever you have that nightmare about space clowns who try to step on you with their giant red shoes!"

"Hey, that hasn't happened since I stopped drinking soda before bedtime— Wait, you hear that?"

"Look, I don't care if we're AlienSlayers, solo libres, or normal, boring kids. So long as we're still friends."

"Well, sorry, but in my book, friends don't lie to each other. You guys lied." Alex looked at Herbert. "*Both* of you."

"I know," Sammi continued. "Then we came clean and apologized." Sammi pointed to Herbert. "And you know what he did when the Klapthorians wanted your head? He lied again. He said he was you—and let them take him."

Alex looked at Herbert.

Herbert shrugged. "You were late, *as usual.*"

Sniffle.

Everyone turned around. Old Man Alex was standing behind them, trying to hold back his tears. When he noticed them looking at him, he burst out blubbering like a giant, pear-shaped baby. He could barely get his words out past his streaming eyes and snotty nose.

"Alex (*sniffle!*), I know they didn't act like very good friends in the past (*snort!*). But they apologized! And Herbert risked his life, because that's what friends do! (*SKRONK!*) But friends also forgive each other! You walk away from friends like that and you'll end up all alone in a cave on the dark side of the moon!"

SPPPLLLLORF!

The bigger, older Alex blew his nose into his sleeve and took a deep, calming breath.

"Take it from me—going solo isn't all that great."

Outside, neither the human Merwinsvillians in the stands nor the G'Dalien Merwinsvillians on the ground dared go near the building where the AlienSlayers and that horrible creature had disappeared. It was quiet, and they feared the worst.

The entire Flee-a-seum was silent. All eyes were fixed upon the bashed-in entrance to the warehouse.

But not for long.

A dark shadow fell over the oblong-shaped building at the end of the Flee-a-seum. It spread like black ink across the entire field, spilling over the G'Daliens' heads, darkening the stands where the human Merwinsvillians stood, and covering the Mayor and his TransPodium. Everyone slowly looked up.

The Klapthorian Death Cruiser was larger than the stadium it hovered over. In fact, it practically blocked out the sun.

"CITIZENS OF MERWINSVILLE!" the Klapthorian captain's voice suddenly echoed off the steep bleachers of the Flee-a-seum. *"ONE OF YOUR OWN HAS FOOLISHLY INSULTED, DISRESPECTED, AND JUST REALLY, REALLY UPSET ME FOR THE LAST*

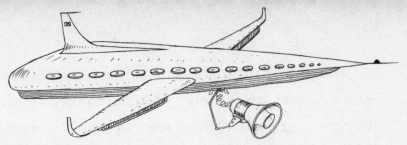

TIME! PREPARE TO HAVE YOUR STADIUM, YOUR CITY, AND YOUR PLANET ANNIHILATED—ROUGHLY IN THAT ORDER."

All eyes looked from the ominous Death Cruiser to Mayor CROM-WELL standing on the tiny TransPodium for some sign of what to do. The great mayor suddenly jumped behind Special Agent Illinois and attempted to hide beneath his long trench coat.

To the crowd, that was as good a sign as any.

The entire population of Merwinsville, humans and G'Daliens alike, burst into total chaos. They screamed, ran in circles, and bumped into one another—until they heard the booming voice again.

"YOUR ONLY HOPE TO AVOID DESTRUCTION IS TO GIVE ME THE ONE YOU CALL . . . EL SOLO LIBRE."

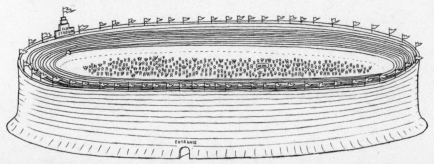

The mixed population of Merwinsville traded looks of confusion. Some muttered to themselves. Others shrugged. The booming voice boomed again, startling them.

"THE REAL ONE THIS TIME! HAND HIM OVER AND YOU SHALL BE SPARED. YOU HAVE SEVENTEEN MILLION, THREE THOUSAND, FOUR HUNDRED EIGHTY-SIX KLAPTHORIAN SNARB-TICKS TO PRESENT HIM TO ME. THIS ROUGHLY TRANSLATES TO ABOUT FIVE EARTH MINUTES. STARTING . . . NOW."

A small G'Dalien toddler sitting on his father's shoulders pointed to the oblong-shaped building at the end of the field.

"Hey, look!"

A lone, pear-shaped figure stepped out of the warehouse wearing a flour sack cape, Mexican wrestling mask, and, over his sweatpants, a pair of tighty-whities.

Very tight tighty-whities.

" *D* O NOT MOCK ME, CHUBBY ONE. I AM IN NO MOOD TO BE MOCKED."

"I *am* El Solo Libre," Old Man Alex declared sternly.

"*WOW. YOU'VE REALLY LET YOURSELF GO IN THE LAST COUPLE OF SNARB-TICKS.*"

Old Man Alex glanced over his shoulder and spotted three silver-dressed humans sneaking from the warehouse building toward the back exit of the Flee-a-seum.

"Yeah, I guess you could say I have."

"SERIOUSLY. GIVE ME THE REAL EL SOLO LIBRE IF YOU WANT TO LIVE. DON'T MAKE ME BE THE BAD GUY HERE."

"I told you, I'm El Solo Libre," Old Man Alex said firmly. "*We all are.*"

"I KNEW HUMANS WEREN'T THE MOST LUMINANT BALLS OF RADIANT PLASMA IN ALL THE WEXLARIAN NEBULAE, BUT THIS IS RIDICULOUS. TRY TO WRAP YOUR PUNY BRAIN AROUND THIS, TUBBY—BY DEFINITION, YOU CAN'T ALL BE SOLO. THINK ABOUT IT. I'LL GIVE YOU A FEW MILLENNIA."

Cruel laughter from the captain and his officers echoed across the Flee-a-seum. The humans booed. A few hurled oversize collectible Flee-Festival cups at the hovering invaders.

"OH, THAT'S REAL ADVANCED OF YOU, GUYS. OKAY. YOU NOW HAVE APPROXIMATELY THREE EARTH MINUTES LEFT TO GIVE ME THE REAL SLAYER BEFORE I UNLEASH MY PET DEATH SLUG ON THIS HUNK OF ROCK YOU CALL HOME."

"And you have just *two* earth minutes left to slap that flying *shrimp boat* into reverse and back on outta our orbital system before we go MoonBat-crazy on you and your little pet—you got that, *shrimp-onna-stick?*"

"*Oooooooooooooooh . . .*" The crowd taunted and cheered from the stands, but stopped as a small panel suddenly slid open near the nose of the ship. The G'Daliens on the ground clustered together, and all eyes watched as the tiny-but-menacing Klapthorian captain emerged from the Death Cruiser.

No one noticed three baggy-skinned G'Daliens who waddled into the Flee-a-seum and stood at the back of the crowd.

The captain buzzed down to Old Man Alex, his officers by his side. His bright yellow, lidless eyes studied the underwear-clad 110-year-old in the Mexican wrestling mask. He burst out into high-pitched, elflike laughter.

"*Heeheeheeheeheeheeheehee!*" he cackled. The others joined in, until the captain held up a sticklike arm, stopping them short. He turned to the crowd.

"This elderly roly-poly human has chosen your entire planet's destiny. And now you will face the horrifyingly destructive force of *Mr. Nibbles*."

The insect aliens buzzed up and perched themselves on Mayor CROM-WELL's TransPodium, where Special Agent Illinois stood beside his son,

wishing he had an oversize rolled up newspaper. As he considered how to single-handedly tackle the space bugs, he heard a sudden incoming transmission on Chicago's HoloWatch.

It was EL-ROY. He spoke in a hushed tone, despite looking very excited. *"Gray Blob to Red Leader, reporting in!"*

"Yes, *Gray Blob!*" Chicago whispered back to the hologram. *"I read you! What've you got?"*

"I'm at the rendezvous point with Dallas and

Sausalito—er, I mean, Meathead and Side of Fries! *Operation Slugwalker Switcheroo, ready to move out!"*

"Okay. I have no idea what that is."

"Look down the field, at the big slug shed!"

Chicago peered past the Klapthorians to the opposite end of the field. He spotted EL-ROY leaning out the hole of the warehouse Mr. Nibbles crashed into, wildly waving his tentacles.

"What are you doing?!"

"Just get down here! We need your help with this thing!"

Chicago looked at his dad, and the two of them silently slipped off the back of the platform, revealing Mayor CROM-WELL, rolled up in a ball under his bodyguard's long trench coat.

"Excuse me." GOR-DON stepped over the mayor as he cautiously approached the Klapthorians, who were waiting for the show to begin. "Hi. Big fan. Love your work."

"Who are you?" the captain barked. There was something about this G'Dalien that looked familiar. Perhaps his makeup.

"A friend. You obviously have this well under control, but I have some information you might

be interested in. Bit of a speed bump, actually. Just before you made your *very* impressive entrance, your 'pet' crash-landed, disappearing into that warehouse over there. He hasn't emerged, and I fear you might be in need of a backup plan. Now, I'm quite an evil plan-maker myself, and I'd be happy to offer my assistance, in exchange for absolute control of the planet—once you're done destroying it, of course."

"*ROAR! GROWL! SNARL! SNORT!*"

Odd noises from inside the building suddenly grabbed their attention. The captain looked back at GOR-DON.

"Are all inhabitants of this planet overweight and stupid?"

"Heeheeheeheeheehee!"

The tittering aliens turned and stared out at the field as the giant Death Slug came waddling out of the warehouse. It bounced along oddly, growling and snarling as it approached the G'Daliens gathered on the floor of the Flee-a-seum. Old Man Alex saw it and ran in terror, straight into the stands of frightened humans.

The Klapthorian captain settled onto his perch on the TransPodium. His black beak widened into a twisted grin.

"Ooh, *this is gonna be good.*"

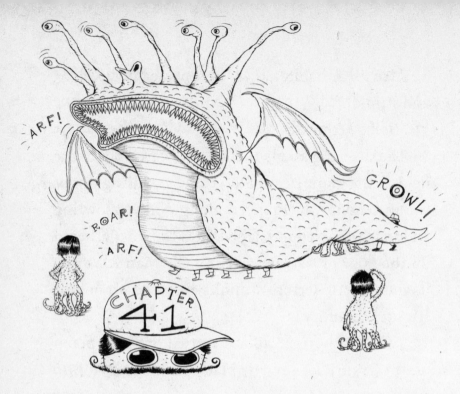

"GROWL! ROAR! ARF! ARF! SNARL!"

"Sir," the first officer asked the Klapthorian captain. "Does Mr. Nibbles seem . . . all right to you?"

At that moment a slight breeze seemed to push the bouncing Death Slug off balance, and it nearly toppled over for no apparent reason.

"He's . . . just a bit groggy. Poor fellah's nap was interrupted. He'll gobble up a few members of this chubby species and be his old horrible self again."

"He seems to have sprouted . . . *tiny feet*, sir."

They both peered at the monster bobbing along unsteadily toward the masses. Each time Mr. Nibbles bounced off the ground, they'd glimpse three pairs of sneakers, a pair of government-issue Special Agent black patent leather shoes, and a dozen or so tentacles, all shuffling madly beneath him.

"Aww, he's *evolving!*" the captain said, sounding like a proud mother. "They grow up so fast, don't they?"

"*HYAAAAAAA!!*"

A loud, angry karate cry suddenly rang out from the group of huddling G'Daliens. The captain and his officers looked down.

"*HO! HAAAAA!*"

One of the three baggy-skinned G'Daliens suddenly ran straight at Mr. Nibbles. She leaped into the air and delivered a devastating horizontal roundhouse kick to the belly of the beast. It rippled like a bowl of Jell-O, and the beast wobbled back and forth as his G'Dalien attacker bounced off, backflipping in the air and landing solidly on her feet.

"*HUP! HUP! HUP-HUP! HUP! HUP!*"

The other two baggy-skinned G'Daliens ran around either side of the wobbly Death Slug and jumped him from behind. One bounce-scaled up the back of Mr. Nibbles and delivered a forearm smash to the top of his head before grabbing Mr. Nibbles' leathery wings and pinning them behind the beast's back.

CLICK! Something was quickly clasped to the beast's wings. As Chicago, his dad, EL-ROY, Dallas, and Sausalito snuck away from beneath the bouncing beastie, the two baggy-skinned G'Daliens hopped off to join the third one on the ground.

All three turned to face the huddling G'Dalien crowd.

"My fellow citizens," the first G'Dalien cried out in a remarkably Sammi-like voice. "Earlier you heard the AlienSlayers admit they were frauds, and that they were never able to protect us!"

The other two saggy-baggy G'Daliens turned to each other.

"We did?"

"But we don't need anyone's protection! We can stand up for ourselves! Are we going to flee, or are we going to fight? I say we let these bullies know they picked the wrong planet to push around!"

The group of G'Daliens stared up at the Klapthorian Winged Death Slug sagging before them. The older ones remembered how this beast (or one just like him) chased them from their home planet fifty years ago. The younger ones thought about the scary stories they'd heard hundreds of times growing up.

A very old grandpa G'Dalien hobbled out of the still-huddled crowd, right up to Mr. Nibbles. He lifted his cane and poked the belly of the wobbly Death Slug.

The old G'Dalien smiled and turned back to face the others.

"Why, he ain't nothin' but a big, blobby bag of bully blubber! *I say let's get him!*"

In an instant, the entire G'Dalien population of Merwinsville burst into cheers and sprung into action. They leaped, climbed, and swarmed all over Mr. Nibbles. The three baggy-skinned G'Daliens stood back and motioned to a floating AirChair high above the Death Slug's head. Suddenly, Mr. Nibbles began rising above the ground, its wings flapping limply.

The G'Daliens hung on, kicking, biting, and scratching the beast as it tried to "fly" away. It rose higher, until it was directly in front of the TransPodium, where the captain and his Klapthorian first officers stood watching in horror.

"Uh, sir? Do you have any orders? *Sir?*"

The Klapthorian leader stared at his pet beastie getting wailed on by peace-loving G'Daliens.

"*Ek.*"

Down below, the three baggy-skinned G'Daliens again gestured to the AirChair—this time in a cutting motion.

CLICK! WHOOSH . . . BOINNNNNGGG!

Mr. Nibbles dropped to the field, causing the

attacking G'Daliens to tumble off him. His body hit the ground with a wobbly *BOING!* and bounced straight back up like a beach ball. It SLAMMED into the TransPodium, knocking the captain and his officers into the air. They took flight and hovered above the field, watching in horror as Mr. Nibbles plummeted back down.

The G'Daliens scattered to avoid being squashed, except one: the old grandpa G'Dalien stood his ground and held his cane over his head, pointy end first. As the blobby Klapthorian Winged Death Slug landed squarely on top of him, the old alien yelled out some sort of ancient G'Dalien battle cry:

"ODELLLIIIDELLLAAAYHIIIIIDLLEH!"

KA-BOOOM!

Mr. Nibbles burst into a million scraps, popping like a giant balloon.*

*Which, technically, he was.

Rubbery pieces of him flew everywhere, in all directions at once, spraying the crowd of humans in the stands, who cheered their fellow citizens on.

Nibbles chunks smacked the hovering captain and his officers, slamming them against the side of their ship. Panicked, they quickly scrambled back into the cockpit and sealed the doors.

"Get us out of here!" the captain cried. *"FULL REVERSE!"*

As the enormous ship began to lift away, Old Man Alex joined forces with the humans in the stands. Together they grabbed a large, floppy chunk of Mr. Nibbles and pulled the stretchy skin like a giant rubber band. As the ship backed away above them, every man, woman, and child in the stands yanked with all their might, *strrrrrrrrrrrrrrretching* it tighter . . . tighter . . . tighter . . .

SPROING!!!

The rubbery chunk flew high above the Flee-a-seum and smacked the tiny windshield of the Klapthorian Death Cruiser with a *THWACK!*

"AAAAUUUUGGGHHHH!" Inside the cockpit, the captain and his officers squealed in horror as the stretched-out googly eye of Mr. Nibbles stared grotesquely at them through the window. *"They're attacking us with the tattered flesh of our own pets! These Merwinsvillians are monsters! RETREAT! RETREAT!"*

The Klapthorian Death Cruiser clumsily turned and thrust upward. It slammed into the top tower of the Flee-a-seum and fishtailed across the Merwinsville skyline. Its massive rear hull swung wildly toward City Hall. *KERRRASH!* The ship wiped out the SlayerLair, smashing its giant windows and lopping off its roof. From the Flee-a-seum the crowd could just make out a large, black, supercomputer-shaped object go soaring across the sky.

"Isn't this just *peachy*," SarcasmaTron said as he sailed toward a large dumpster in an alley on the other side of town.

The mighty cruiser straightened out and blasted skyward, fleeing the earth as fast as it could. As it headed back into space, all the citizens of Merwinsville, human and G'Dalien, burst into a loud and hearty cheer—this time in honor of themselves.

CHAPTER 42

The Merwinsvillians were so busy high-fiving each other, no one noticed as Old Man Herbert drifted down in his AirChair and joined in the celebration with the other members of *Operation Slugwalker Switcheroo*. Also going unnoticed were the three baggy-skinned G'Daliens, waddling toward the Flee-a-seum exit.

They almost made it.

Mayor CROM-WELL was not one to allow local heroes to go unrecognized, especially when they deserved loud, public mayoral thanks. Spotting them from up on the TransPodium, he bellowed so all could hear: "THOSE THREE ARE GETTING AWAY!" His voice boomed through the arena to the crowd below. "QUICK! ENTHUSIASTICALLY SEIZE THEM!"

The crowd swarmed the three frumpy G'Daliens, lifted them up onto their shoulders, and carried them back to the center of the field. As the heroes were jostled and bounced into the air by the happy crowd, their three rubber G'Dalien heads suddenly popped off. The cheers of joy turned to screams of horror—until all eyes recognized the faces of

Sammi, Alex, and Herbert in their rubber suits. The crowd fell silent.

"It was you?!" someone yelled out from the crowd.

"Wait," said another. "You said you weren't AlienSlayers."

The three looked at one another, unsure of what to tell them.

Alex spoke up. "We're not AlienSlayers! We're not Solo Libres, we're not superheroes. We're just . . . *friends*."

Sammi grinned at him and added, "You're the ones who slayed that space slug, not us! What I said was true—you don't need to flee, and you don't need anyone else to fight your battles for you!"

The two of them gave Herbert a look. He was staring off sadly at the craggy wreckage of what was the SlayerLair, now the lopped-off top of City Hall. Alex elbowed him in the ribs.

"*Ow!* Uh, that's right. You all ripped apart a giant, slug-shaped balloon. So, yeah—way to go."

There was a half second of silence—then the crowd erupted once again in a burst of civic pride.

The human Merwinsvillians made their way down from the stands and waded into the celebration on the field. GOR-DON searched the waves of people, looking for Marion. When he spotted her from a distance, her eyes grew wide. She burst into a sprint, running straight for him. *At last*, GOR-DON thought to himself. He shut his eyes, spread his arms, and puckered up for a kiss as best he could, considering he didn't have lips.

POW! "*HIIIIYYYYYAAAAHHHH!!*"

Marion plowed into GOR-DON and launched herself off his stubbly bald head. She shot into the air, her steady, warriorlike gaze fixed on something just beyond the crowd of G'Daliens holding up Sammi, Alex, and Herbert.

"RRRRREEEEEEEOOOOOOOOOOAAAARRRR!!"

The *real* Mr. Nibbles had CRASHED out of the front of the oblong warehouse and stretched its powerful wings, bursting out of its Lunar Shuttle straitjacket. It launched into the air and dove straight for the three snack-sized humans responsible for disturbing his nap and giving him a pounding headache—Sammi, Alex, and Herbert.

Mayor CROM-WELL fainted.

"Sweet chariots of fire!" Special Agent Illinois leaped up onto the TransPodium, dove on his chubby boss, and immediately gave him mouth-to-mouth resuscitation, despite the fact that they both had mustaches, and the mayor had eaten an egg-salad sandwich for lunch.

Marion soared over the mob. She ripped the hairnet from her head and slammed midair into the angry worm. In an instant she stretched her hairnet around the tip of the Death Slug's snout. The G'Daliens below dropped the ex-slayers on the ground and scattered as Marion swung herself up onto Mr. Nibbles' neck and pulled back on the hairnet with all her might, like a crazed, lunch lady cowgirl yanking the reins of a wild stallion.

"RRRRREEEEEEEOOOOOOOOOOAAAARRRR!!"

The leather-winged beast swooped out of its dive, missing Sammi, Alex, and Herbert by a hair. Mr. Nibbles soared back up and bucked madly above the field. The Merwinsvillians still in the stands cheered like fans at an alien rodeo, while those on the ground joined the G'Daliens jumping up and down wildly at the spectacle overhead. Marion held on with one hand, the other raised high, riding the bucking Death Slug as it thrashed about above the field.

Finally Mr. Nibbles crashed to the ground and skidded to a halt, its belly heaving as he tried to catch his breath. Marion leaned forward and rubbed his head, cooing softly in his ear.

"Easy, big fellah. Mama's here now."

The crowd went wild, rushing up to Marion as she dismounted. They lifted her up over their heads and paraded her around as EL-ROY, Dallas, and Sausalito ran to tie down the broken and defeated Klapthorian Death Slug.

Still lying in the dirt nearby, GOR-DON watched the entire scene in amazement. A slight grin grew on his lipless mouth.

"What a woman," he mumbled to himself. "GOR-DON *likey . . .*"

"So, m'lady. We meet again."

GOR-DON looked up. LO-PEZ smiled as his tentacles were doing various things at the same time—fixing his hair, smoothing his mustache, checking his breath, opening a bag of salt 'n' vinegar potato chips. His caterpillar eyebrows began doing push-ups again, double-time.

"I believe this belongs to you, *m'lady*." His one free tentacle held GOR-DON's trampled, dirty blonde wig as if it were a delicate lace hankie and gently placed it atop his stubbly head.

"You've gotta be kidding me," GOR-DON grumbled.

The ex-AlienSlayers stood back and watched the massive celebration: people and G'Daliens hugging, dancing, and spraying one another with bright green soda pop.

A pear-shaped figure pushed his way through the gyrating crowd with a big grin on his face. Old Man Alex had taken off the Mexican wrestling mask his Uncle Davey had brought back from Guadalupe, and what little hair he had on his head was sticking out in all directions.

"Did you guys see that?! We sent those shrimp

bugs packing!"

"I don't believe my eyes," a voice said. "You found him . . ." Old Man Herbert floated up in his AirChair. *"Fraidy-Cat Filby!"*

"Uh, sorry if I don't know your name. I played a mind-numbing video game for fifty years, and I'm slowly regaining my memory."

"That's quite all right. It's good to see you're well."

"Thanks! I was gone for a while. Hiding out on the—"

"The dark side of the moon, I know. Did you get the cave-warming gift I sent you?"

"Ah-ha!"

Young Alex stepped up and poked a finger at the elderly inventor. "So you *did* send him that video game system! I knew it!"

Old Man Alex looked genuinely surprised.

"Why would I do that? Those things rot your brain. I sent him a SuperCheezyFrankOnnaStickerator 3000."

"You *said* you had no idea where he went," Herbert said.

"I didn't—not at first. But years later, when I heard he ran into trouble and disappeared, I used

293

an early prototype of SarcasmaTron to locate him.

"Then, remembering his love for those nasty stick-dogs, I invented a machine that would keep him fed for as long as he wished to stay hidden, and I sent it to him anonymously."

"Bio-vapor CO_2 reverse thermo-protein conden-senator?" young Herbert asked. The old inventor nodded. "Nice."

"Wait," Alex said suspiciously. "If that's true, why didn't you just tell me where to find him?"

"I wanted to test my theory of intersecting parallel-event paths," Old Man Herbert said. "And by finding yourself, you helped me prove that they exist!"

Old Man Alex stepped up and gave Old Man Herbert an enormous bear hug, almost pulling him off his AirChair. "I knew I recognized a friend," he said.

"Aw," Sammi interjected. "See? You two are best friends, even in parallel-event paths!"

"Nice story, old man," Alex suddenly said, pulling his older self off Herbert's older self. "But it doesn't explain why you wrote this note and sent it along with that brainwashing AlienSlayer43:

Virtual Vengeance game! HA!"

He shoved it into Old Man Herbert's face. Everyone crowded around and looked closely at it.

"Look at the bottom! *Your old friend and neighbor, "H.S."'* Let's hear your 'theory' on *that*!"

Old Man Herbert pushed it back. "That's not my handwriting."

"Pff." Alex rolled his eyes.

Sammi peered closer at the note. "No," she said slowly. "He's telling the truth. I don't know how this could possibly be, but I recognize that handwriting. It's *mine*."

Another memory suddenly trickled into Old Man Alex's brain. He looked at the note, the handwriting, Sammi's face.

Click.

"*H.S.—Hammy Sammi!*" he exclaimed. "My old next-door neighbor! Now I remember! We gave each other *rhyming food nicknames!*" He looked over at the two Herberts. "And *Sherbet Herbert!* I knew I recognized you guys!"

Sammi, Alex, and Herbert said goodbye to Old Man Alex and Old Man Herbert, leaving them reminiscing about old times together.

"Looks like our parallel-event-path selves were friends, too," Sammi said. "Kinda nice to know."

"Well, obviously our event path lives are far superior to theirs," Herbert said. "I mean, *rhyming food nicknames?* Who does that?"

"Don't complain," Alex said. "*Alex Shallots?* That doesn't even rhyme!"

The sun was low in the sky over the empty streets of Future Merwinsville as they exited the Flee-a-seum without anyone noticing or caring. They stopped and looked back at the happy, celebrating citizens of Future Merwinsville.

"So if my observations are accurate," Herbert said, "the entire city of Merwinsville just saved *their own AlienSlayers from being horribly devoured by an actual alien.*"

"It's more than we ever did," Sammi answered.

"Once again, ironic."

"I guess they don't need us anymore." Sammi smiled.

"Let's face it," Alex said. "They never did."

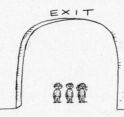

At the top of the museum steps, Sammi, Alex, and Herbert watched the sun set over Future Merwinsville one last time. Fireworks blasted in the distant sky over the Flee-a-seum.

"Best Flee-Festival ever," Alex said.

Soon the three ex–AlienSlayers were making their way slowly down the Hallway of Human History. When they came to the caveman diorama, they were surprised to find Chicago standing dutifully in front of the fake cave.

"I gave EL-ROY the day off," he said with a shrug.

"Good," Herbert said. "I don't think we could survive another operation under his team leadership."

"So, is this it? I mean, forever?"

"Not forever," Herbert said. "We'll all be back in a century or so. We're gonna come back old school. *We'll age*."

"You're not gonna get all weepy on us are you?" Alex asked.

"*No*," Chicago shot back. "If I ever wanna have some *real* adventures, I can always hang out with your 110-year-old selves."

"Not mine," Sammi said.

Chicago smiled at her. "Hey, I'm sorry I was such a jerk. I didn't mean to—I mean, I—I'm just gonna miss you. Not the fans, TV interviews, or the SkyLimo, but you."

"We know," Alex said. "That's why we're trusting you to wait here after we go through—for one last mission."

"I don't understand."

"You will," Sammi said as she hit the switch on her N.E.D. suit. Alex and Herbert did the same. The wormhole came to life, its blue swirling glow lighting up Sammi's face.

She leaned away from the force pulling her back to the present—and gave Chicago a kiss on the cheek.

"See ya around, FutureBoy."

She turned to Alex and Herbert. All together the three of them grabbed their noses and cannonballed into the swirling blue vortex.

FOOMPF! FOOMPF! FOOMPF!

Herbert, Alex, and Sammi disappeared into the wormhole, leaving Chicago standing alone, wondering what his last task for the AlienSlayers could possibly be.

Sammi, Alex, and Herbert were still laughing as they tumbled out of the wormhole and onto the grass. Standing over them was Alex's mother, with Ellie and Mr. Snookybuns at her side. And they all looked very upset.

"Alex," Mrs. Filby said sternly. "You directly disobeyed me by playing this spaceman game, you lied to your father about going camping, and—"

"Excuse me, Mrs. Filby?" Sammi said, cutting her off. "I know Alex disobeyed you, but for what it's worth, the only reason he did it was to help Herbert and me."

Alex and Herbert looked at Sammi and wondered where she was going with this.

"See, Herbert and I weren't being very honest friends to Alex. And we were being such jerks that the only way he could show us how friends should treat one another was to play our game with us one last time."

Mrs. Filby looked suspiciously at the three silver-suited, soon-to-be sixth graders. "Herbert. Is this true?"

Herbert was silent for a moment. Sammi glared at him. Finally, he nodded. "Yes, Mrs. Filby. Alex's demonstration of friendship has proven to be surprisingly enlightening."

"Well, Alex. I must say, that's very—uh, *normal-sounding* praise from your friends. I suppose if these are the kinds of things you're sharing and learning with your spaceman game, it wouldn't be so bad if you continued to play it."

Ellie's eyes narrowed. She slowly squeezed Mr. Snugglebuns' head in frustration.

"That's okay, Mom," Alex said. "This was our last mission. We're taking off our silver suits and packing them off to a place where we won't see them for a long, long time."

"Oh. Well, that's very mature of you, Alex," Mrs. Filby said, slightly surprised. She got a thought and added, "Now that you'll have some free time, I may need your help in getting your father to quit video games. I think he might have a problem. We'll talk at dinner."

Alex, Sammi, and Herbert watched Mrs. Filby lead Ellie and Mr. Snugglebuns into the house. Without saying a word, they stood up and unzipped their N.E.D. suits. Standing in their normal, boring kid clothes, they gently folded the silver suits and climbed the ladder to the mouth of the tube slide.

"Well, here goes nothing," Sammi said.

"You mean *everything*," Herbert corrected her.

"All righty," Alex said as he flicked on the suit in his hands. "AlienSlayers, start your engines!"

A tiny blue swirl inside the slide began to pulse and come to life. Herbert flipped his on. The tiny blue swirl got bigger and stronger. Sammi smiled and flipped hers on, too.

WUBBA-WUBBA-WUBBA-WUBBA-WUBBA-WUBBA!!

The wormhole surged. The empty N.E.D. suits jerked in their arms, lurching toward the wide

mouth of the slide. The three neighbors looked at one another.

"ONE! TWO! THREE! GO!" They let go of their suits.

FOOMPF! FOOMPF! FOOMPF!

In the blink of an eye, the three silver N.E.D. suits, the keys to Sammi's, Alex's, and Herbert's wormhole, disappeared. And a half a blink later, so did the wormhole itself.

The three of them sat there for a moment in silence.

Herbert got up first. He slowly climbed down the ladder without saying a word. Sammi followed.

"Yeeeehaaawww!"

They turned to the bottom of the tube slide and watched as Alex tumbled out onto the grass.

"Y'know, this is actually a pretty cool jungle gym."

"Well, I guess I'll see you guys at school," Herbert said.

"I hear sixth grade is pretty challenging," Sammi added.

"Hope we can handle it," Alex said, doing his best SarcasmaTron imitation.

Alex, Sammi, and Herbert burst out laughing. The three ex-AlienSlayers walked off in three separate directions toward their three separate houses, giggling to themselves.

Chicago Illinois sat cradled in the tusks of the large, stuffed woolly mammoth, tossing pebbles at the black-painted cave entrance. The last pebble bounced off the fake rock, and the entrance began to glow and swirl a deep blue. He sat up.

POP! POP! POP!

Three silver objects suddenly shot out of the cave hole and smacked him in the head. Chicago fell out of his mammoth hammock. He pulled the empty N.E.D. suits off his head, looked down at them, and smiled proudly as he realized exactly what his friends had entrusted him to do.

At the opposite end of the Hallway of Human History, Chicago approached a large-handled bin in the wall. Above it was a sign:

TRASH DISINTEGRATOR CHUTE. Chicago pulled open the bin door and looked down the dark shaft.

He held the three N.E.D. suits and took just a second to contemplate what he was about to do. He made a silent little wish that Alex, Sammi, and Herbert would live a long and happy life, so that someday he could see them again.

Then he quickly stuffed the suits into the bin.

He didn't watch them fall down the chute but rather quickly slammed the bin lid closed. He knew himself too well—if he thought about it too much, he might change his mind and dive after them, keeping just one for himself so he could visit the friends he would miss very much.

Chicago Illinois wiped away a tear with his sleeve and walked out of the Merwinsville Museum of Human History.

GOR-DON thanked LO-PEZ for the lift home, promised to call him sometime, then wiped the mud and makeup off his face as soon as the confused and chubby G'Dalien sped away in the mayor's sleek SkyLimo.

"*Idiot*," he seethed. He slogged into the museum and approached the door to his toxic waste closet home.

CLANG!

The sound echoed from above, through the disintegration chute, which emptied into the trash pit outside his front door. GOR-DON leaned over the pit and looked up the dark chute.

FLOOMPH!

A large clump of silver material dropped out of the chute, covering his face. Freaking out, he fell over the railing to the pit but shot a tentacle out to keep himself from falling into the laser-disintegration unit below. The silver heap slipped off his head. His other tentacle shot down and grabbed it.

GOR-DON heaved his blobby butt over the railing and he looked at the N.E.D. suits in his tiny, clawlike hands.

"They get all the glory, while I get their dirty laundry." He wobbled over to his toxic closet door and shuffled inside.

"You've got issues," the pleasant computer voice announced.

"Tell me about it," he replied as he dropped the suits on his desk. A new headline beamed onto his wall of holo-clippings.

"Oh, Marion," the heartbroken G'Dalien moaned. "How did things go so horribly, horribly wrong?"

"That's easy. You let your feelings *get in the way of your* duty . . ."

The croaky old voice startled GOR-DON. He stood up and looked around the room.

"Y-Your Mightiness?!" GOR-DON stuttered as he tried to act pleasantly surprised. "It's been years! How have you been?"

"You failed me, janitor. *Again.*"

"No, no! I did everything you asked all those years ago! I delivered your package to the cave on the dark side of the moon, I trained the MoonBats to keep watch over his cave, *everything*! Do you know how hard it is to train a MoonBat *in the dark?!*"

"And yet . . . *he came back.*"

"Well, if I may make a small suggestion, in all your wisdom and evil ingeniousness, I think perhaps you may have underestimated his *friends*..."

"*His friends?!* You dare question *my* authority on his *friends*?! I'm quite aware of what his friends are capable of..."

GOR-DON flinched as the shadowy figure approached from the darkness and stepped into the green glow of the holo-clippings on the wall.

"After all, *I used to be one of them.*"

The old woman had long, silver-and-black streaked hair and wore a dark bodysuit with a flowing black cape.

She sneered at him and turned to the newest holo-clipping. Then she noticed the clump of N.E.D. suits lying on the desk, and picked them up.

"Where did you get these?"

"Oh, I caught them in the disintegration chute. I suppose the AlienSlayers have retired. So that's good, right?"

She looked back at GOR-DON and began to laugh. GOR-DON laughed with her, nervously. She aimed a fist at the holo-clipping wall. Her large silver bracelet began to glow a brilliant blue.

"You've done well, janitor. I think you've earned a little getaway."

"Oh. Where am I going?"

"Not 'where,' but 'when.'"

"I'm afraid I don't know what you're—"

"You don't need to know anything right now, janitor. Except how to sew."

"What? I can't sew—"

WHUMPH! The silver clump of N.E.D. suits hit GOR-DON in the head.

"Learn."

KABLAM!!

Her bracelet emitted a powerful ball of blue light, which blew a massive hole in the thick wall of GOR-DON's room. He pulled the N.E.D. suits from his face to see smoke and debris swirl and scatter all around him. When it settled, he looked up.

Old Lady Sammi Clementine had left the building.